THE MURDER
BOOK

The Murder Book

Copyright © 2018 Barbara Marvin
ISBN: 978-1-949109-023
Imprint: Anchor Book Press
440 W. Colfax Street, Unit 1132,
Palatine, IL 60078
Printed in the United States

THE MURDER BOOK

by Barbara Marvin

Anchor Book Press · Palatine

Other Books
by
Barbara Marvin

Unfinished Business

Deceptive Business

Acknowledgement:

Writing this book has been fun and difficult at the same time. Thanks to my publisher, Anchor Book Press, for keeping me on schedule. Looking forward to a lasting relationship.

Dedication:

This book is dedicated to my sister, Sandy, who looks forward to reading a good mystery.

"Murder is like potato chips: you can't stop with just one."
— Stephen King, *Under the Dome*

Chapter 1

Cole drank a little more than he had planned, but hey, he had a lot to celebrate. For a young man in his early thirties he was going places. This was the beginning. His book had been published, the first of many, he thought. His publisher had secured a contract with a local bookstore for an author signing event.

He flopped on the sofa and grinned to himself. The future looked good. Maybe he could get out of this crappy apartment. He knew he couldn't afford a condo near Ringling Causeway where his best friend, Jon, lived. Then again, if he wrote a couple of best sellers, maybe he could. It was something to look forward to.

Jon had a lot of experience and his father had a lot of clout. Cole grimaced when he thought of Jon's father because he never knew his father. In all his years his mother, may God rest her soul, had never identified him. Do you know how hard it is growing up without a father? When Cole complained, his mom always said it was easier growing up without a father than it would have been growing up with his father. She wouldn't say much more.

Jon was a journalist and had been instrumental in Cole actually following though with his dream to write. He wondered what first inspired Ernst Hemingway to write. Oh well, that was another story. But, Hemingway was his role model. He had studied pictures of him and read his biography, his objective was to be like him. And, if he looked in the mirror, he could see the resemblance. If he played his cards right he would be the new Ernst Hemingway of Sarasota. Because he would never move to Illinois where Hemingway was born, let alone Key West where Hemingway lived for some time. But the idea was always there.

This would be a week like no other; an interview with a local television station, his biography in the paper thanks to Jon, a book signing, could it get any better than this?

He would hardly have time for his usual evening at Big Bart's. Though he knew he would make time for that. After all, Jon deserved his company. He was the one that helped him make this dream come true.

He expected a few copies of his books to arrive tomorrow, he would sign them and share them, for free, with Jon and his friends at Bart's. Those crazy guys had helped also, even if they didn't know it. He laughed out loud, wondering if most of them could even read a novel.

"I don't know if I can sleep tonight," he murmured to himself.

As he raised himself off the sofa to see what leftovers were in the fridge, his phone buzzed.

"Yeah," he answered.

"Is this Cole?" the caller asked

"Yeah, who is this?"

"Cole Mitchell?"

"I said yes, what do you want?"

"I understand you have a book ready to hit the stands."

"Yes, I do. Friday is the big day. You can drop by Books-a-Million and get a signed copy. What did you say your name was?"

"Cole, I've got to tell you, you won't make it to Friday. You should have known better than to write everything you might have thought you knew. This is your notice. Good-bye!"

The caller's gravelly voice died as the line went dead, but Cole heard him loud and clear. He didn't recognize him, but at the moment Cole forgot about his future, his fame, and his next book.

Chapter 2

The dazzling sun on Ringling Boulevard was almost blinding for those large blue eyes. Willa entered the building, like she had done for several years, through the revolving doors with energy and vigor, removing her sunglasses with her right hand. Her left arm was near her side, holding her loose fitting jacket close to her body allowing her Glock 17 to be shielded from sight. A habit she had perfected over the years. The feel of the gun was security, warmth. She felt alive and strong. She loved this job.

Pushing through these doors transformed her. She surveyed the lobby. She only wished her personal life permitted her to feel this good. As she walked through the building she tried hard to leave that part of her life behind. A routine she had developed out of necessity.

This was a very secure building having recently been renovated. Bullet-proof glass windows; tinted to keep the glare to a minimum. Video cameras blinking at you from every corner, metal detectors and armed security guards insuring safety.

"Good morning Detective Dupree," the uniformed guard greeted her with his generous smile as she passed through the check point.

"Good morning, Lester. Good to see you back, how is that new baby and your wife doing?"

"Great! I didn't want to come in today, just wanted to sit there and look at the face of my son. He is beautiful." Lester's demeanor had changed at the mention of his son. Willa knew she would never know how that felt and jealousy raised its ugly head, for just a second. She knew Lester would be a great dad, unlike her own.

Her rubber soled shoes made little sound on the stone tiles as she turned left and walked past the elevators to the far corridor of the main floor. This foyer was quiet now but would soon be filled with visitors heading to the many county offices and courtrooms. Turning the corner, she smiled at June, the receptionist, as she swiped her ID card and entered the sheriff's office. She glanced at her partner, Russell Wilson. At six two, 250 pounds, his large frame more than filled his chair. His brown hair; cut short to hide the premature gray at his temples gave him that serious military look. His brown eyes were focused on his computer and her heart fluttered just a beat looking at him. He glanced up and grinned. They worked well as partners and at one time it might have become something more, but now ...

As the lone female detective in this office, she worked twice as hard as anyone here. There had been the usual problems when she started, but now she was a fixture. She had marked her territory with her drive and compulsion. Her therapist said compulsion wasn't an asset, but she never visualized not having that forcible urge, even after years of therapy. She took up martial arts to work out some of her aggressions. It only strengthened her physical abilities; life would never allow her to relax. And her intellect, her purpose in life would never suggest she pursue any other vocation.

Last year this 6-story building had been fully remodeled. After much internal give and take on the part of Captain Dunbar, things looked good in here. The dull, dingy walls had lost their standing and became a neutral off-white. Metal desks had been replaced with dark oak and bulletin boards had been added in strategic spots to accommodate the many projects now on the agenda. Lisa, the media expert, had insisted on a "wall of fame" that boasted new pictures and snapshots of the sheriffs and detectives, as they protected the public. She had increased the public awareness of this office to the point that was hard to match in even larger offices. In many cities and towns, the 'blue uniform' was disrespected. She never wanted that to be the case here. She took it very seriously.

After several hours of quiet concentration, Willa peered over her computer at Lisa hard at work. "Hey Lisa."

"Yeah, what's up?" Lisa answered. Lisa had been with the office longer than Willa, as community affairs director. Captain Dunbar hired her when he realized the world was changing and he needed someone to stand in front of the media, someone good looking and smart who knew just how to rebuff unwanted probing when it was necessary.

She was all that and more. Lisa brought 15 years of experience, a bachelor's degree in mass communication, and a graduate certificate in criminal justice to the department. She had worked in several much larger offices and cities and created a sophisticated appeal to the job. Her newest project was a public awareness program geared to informing the public about the importance of any new laws. Especially the new national guide "See Something, Say Something". All publicity was her baby, good, bad or indifferent.

"How about writing a release about idiots that fire their guns in the air to celebrate?"

"Sounds like you got the short straw. Anybody hurt?"

"Somebody's dog got killed. Now the neighbor is going to sue. We arrested the shooter; he made bail. Same story, different day," Willa noted and frowned. Although Willa didn't usually get involved in politics, issues with guns were a big problem for the sheriff's department. She was not happy about people using guns as fireworks. Would stricter laws be the answer, she didn't know. Many people thought so, and it seemed to make sense. However, no one knew better than Willa that you can't legislate common sense.

"I'll call Jon Albee; he's always looking for a story." Lisa replied, referring to a hot shot local journalist.

"Yeah, try it, but Jon wants sensational stuff. I don't know if he can get enough mileage out of this." Willa knew Jon Albee from the Sarasota Sentinel and he was good for making a mountain out of a mole hill. His name was all over. And he would listen to any story Lisa had to tell, as long as Lisa was buying the beer; which she sometimes did.

Seeing Lester downstairs had filled Willa with a sense of depression, uncontrollable thoughts of the family she would never have. Try as she might to overcome it, it was always there in the back of her mind. Suddenly, her need for coffee merged with her need to get out of the office. Starbucks across the street was where she could escape temporarily. "Who wants coffee? I'm running to Starbucks," she asked as she rose from her desk. She stretched her shoulders, shook out the kinks and looked at Russell.

"I'll have one," Russell confirmed, and smiled. It was the second time this morning she had seen him smile. But who was counting. That face. Yes, I had better take a break, she thought.

"Kevin?" Willa quipped. "Yes?"

"Well, since you're going, yes," he replied. "And bring me one of those scone things while you are there, if you don't mind."

"Lisa?" Willa looked at Lisa.

"I'll go with you," Lisa announced. "I need to move a little; a chai with a splash of sunshine on my face might help."

"Your face is like sunshine itself, no need for more," Kevin teased.

"Don't you have work to do, Kevin? Catching bad guys or something? Maybe I'll call 'Daddy' and tell him to keep you after school; you are flirting with the help," she laughed.

Kevin laughed, too, but buried his head in his work. The mention of his dad made him cringe. Everyone knew George Vasser, retired detective, was always pushing Kevin to be more aggressive, more vocal, more like himself. His dad had been a good detective and found it difficult to back off his son. Kevin lived every day with that stigma.

Willa motioned towards the door with her head. "Let's do it."

The traffic on Ringling Boulevard had become unyielding at this time of morning. Drivers were impatient and used their horns to let you know. The array of out of state tags was impressive, seemed to be more each year. Willa and Lisa crossed at the corner and headed for their favorite stop.

"Willa, can I ask you something?" Lisa queried, as soon as they got their drinks. Lisa respected Willa and as the only females in an office filled with testosterone, she felt connected to her. She also knew Willa was smart and well respected in the office.

"Sure," Willa answered. "Nothing personal or incriminating, I hope."

"Right, nothing like that," Lisa laughed. "Jon Albee, our favorite journalist, is looking to do a series on our cold cases; he also has a friend that has written a book, fiction. He thinks it might take off with some publicity." She paused, "It just came off the press."

They took their drinks to the back, where the noise level was not too high. The room was filled with more bail bondsmen and possible clients than usual. Willa glanced around and nodded to several lawyers she recognized. "And, what's the problem?" she asked, turning her attention to Lisa.

"Well, he wants some inside info; anything I can give him. He's doing this story and mentoring his friend, helping him come up with some mysteries based on real cold cases." Lisa looked at Willa and paused.

"And?" Willa prodded

"Well cold cases mean they haven't been solved. If he doesn't know about them, I'm not willing to bring them up. Besides, why bring up cases we can't solve or haven't solved. We are trying to improve our image. Not publish our short comings."

"So, what's the problem?" Willa thought she already knew the answer. She wanted Lisa to acknowledge it. She also knew cold cases were on the back burner. They were cold for a reason. No new leads. No new information. They worked them when they could; but as of now there were no real cold case investigations going on. With tight budgets, they weren't likely to get more help to solve them.

"The problem is Jon Albee." She stated as if that was answer enough.

"Ah, so you're trying to keep Jon ... how should I say this? Satisfied, but not exactly in the loop."

"Yes, sort of," Lisa's blue eyes were animated. "But what if Jon were to do a story on old cases... say, with the idea of helping jog someone's memory by presenting a new slant on them."

"That may help us but how can that help his friend?" Willa asked.

"How he helps his friend is his business, not mine, but he has a few ideas. I think his friend's new book is about a cold case, so he'll put a good spin on it. It could help us. I haven't read his book, but maybe I'll ask Jon for a copy."

Willa liked Lisa's idea, and this might work. Lisa was always focused on the department and the detectives. Jon could be a pain, but on the other hand, he had helped many times by publishing things they asked him to. Good public relations were at the top of Lisa's list.

Leaving the coffee shop, they dodged foot traffic that appeared heading for the offices of the bail bondsmen on the other side of the street. Willa recognized a few. She was always surprised at the number of repeat offenders. Today the sun was cooperating with the chamber of commerce's promise of sunshine, with not a cloud in the sky as they trudged back.

The lobby of the County Justice Building had filled up, and there was Lester, smiling as they approached security. He waved them through as they headed back to work. Stepping back into the office Willa felt connected, the coffee had helped.

Willa was a beautiful woman and being able to turn heads sometimes worked to her advantage; being tough always worked in her favor. When she was younger, friends encouraged her to become a model, telling her she had the looks and the stature for it. They never convinced her. She looked in the mirror and saw a face her father hated. She smiled, never telling them about her childhood. If it wasn't for that life, she might have chosen the glamorous job of walking the runways. Now, her passion was seeing the perps walk the runways or as she put it bluntly; seeing the scum pay.

It never ceased to amaze her that she still felt so passionate about putting the guilty away. She often wondered if she felt this anger, this rage at criminals because she was as bad as her dad. Years of therapy had little effect on her. If she was open and comfortable telling her life story, everyone would realize her soul had been scarred for life by the abuse she and her mother received at the hands of her father; a man never far from her subconscious, even long after his death. And to make matters worse, she married a carbon copy of her father.

She thought his kind would be easy to spot, not so. She had made a poor choice when she married. She thought divorce would be her answer, but that only provided a temporary reprieve. Her ex came back to haunt her, but sometimes the gods are looking down, she thought. Her ex-husband was leading a double life and as the ending to bad novel is predictable, so was his. He was murdered by a male lover seeking revenge. As bad as this was, it did put an end to her worrying about what he would do next, but it left her with a lot of baggage.

She shook her head, shaking off any particles of that life in her thoughts. It seemed she would be in therapy for the rest of her life; work was the answer and she did it with a vengeance. "Hey guys, here's your coffee," Willa announced entering the office. "You should see that traffic, where do these people come from?"

Russell looked up. "If you lived up north, you'd want to be here, too. Sunshine, beautiful beaches, beautiful women, and beautiful scenery; law enforcement keeping them safe. What more could they ask for," he laughed. "The polar vortex has gripped most of the country. We are utopia, paradise, heaven on earth, need I say more?"

"Yeah, but if I had my way, they would be required to pass a strenuous driving test before crossing the state line."

Barbara Marvin

Chapter 3

This morning had been a test for Jon Albee. He hadn't left his desk except to head for the break room and back. At least the coffee had a room to itself, unlike the journalists who all sat in a large room with no partitions or dividers. Sometimes he had a difficult time focusing on the issues at hand; today was one of those days. No longer the only media source in town, the primary job was to draw readers. Sales were down because everyone over the age of five had an iPad, tablet or other electronic device for instantaneous news. The paper's financial problems would be the topic of the staff meeting this morning.

For meetings like this, they used the large meeting room. It was well appointed, boasting a heavy maple table with a granite top; a holdover from more prosperous times.

The chairs that surrounded the table were comfortable, upholstered several times yet they still held the feel of luxury. This is where the indulgence ended. The walls were covered with portraits of past heavy hitters in the publishing world. Floor to ceiling windows allowed full sunlight to be tempered with verticals keeping the glare to a minimum. Procedures had changed over the years and the dress code was totally casual.

Jon, dressed in his signature jeans and plaid sport shirt, glanced at Skip Davidson, his boss. Skip looked terrible, must have had another rough night. If Jon were keeping track, lately there were many more than usual.

"Close the door, please." Adele Raymond, the publisher and big boss, said as she smiled. Jon had been around long enough to realize she always smiled when she was about to deliver bad news. Otherwise she was a real hard-ass and never cracked a smile.

She ran a tight ship and her direction was what kept this paper afloat. That, and the fact that she had a great crew. Last year had seen the loss of several seasoned employees and the tightening of the financial belt. Jon hoped they could hold on another year. He enjoyed working here; loved the location and most of the crew was easy to work with. He had worked hard to earn his place at this table.

"Well Jon, good of you to show up," the sarcasm in Skip's voice grated on Jon's nerves. Skip was pointing to his watch.

Jon lifted his left arm, eyed his Rolex and said. "I'm not late, what are you talking about?" Normally, Jon didn't intentionally flaunt it, but he came from money. The watch had been a gift from his father several years ago and Jon knew he was taunting Skip with it now.

"You are usually the first in here." Skip's feeling of envy was about to get the better of him.

"Sit, please Jon." Adele said giving Skip the look and saving Jon further ridicule by his boss.

Jon smiled at her to signify a thanks. Looking around he noticed, he was the last in the room and the last to take a chair.

"I'd like to start this meeting by telling you, all of you, you did a great job last year, and the year was a little better than expected. This coming year is expected to hold its own, with that said... I'll level with you. It will still be a rough one."

Pausing she looked around the table. "As a community focused paper, we don't compete with the giants of the industry," pausing again, she smiled. "We focus on the needs of our local readers, advertisers, and businesses. We are locally owned; we are a small-town publisher and fill the requirements as such. I know you've heard this before. I'm telling you again, we can't lose sight of that. With the expertise each of you bring to this company and with the goal to be better tomorrow than we are today, I expect this will be a good year for us all." The meeting dragged on and she continued to address the changing times and the direction they needed to pursue. Jon's mind was on his own future.

"Jon," Skip was calling his name and he looked up sharply.

"Yeah."

"What's on tap, what's the latest, what's your idea of the next big thing? What are you working on now?" Skip found it easy to pass the buck to Jon.

Jon glanced around the table. Everyone's eyes converged on him. "I'm not sure about the next big thing. Things are fairly quiet now with the holidays over and such. I'm working on a series about local cold cases. The sheriff's department has agreed to open up some things to me," he said stretching the truth just a little. "A local author has written a book inspired by a Sarasota cold case. He writes fiction. My stories might help law enforcement, I hope. I'll alert the public to what really happened. I'll point out and revisit the crime and then ask for help from the public. Play up the local author thing. Go from there."

Adele's carefully styled, bright red hair didn't move as she nodded. "Okay, what else?"

Skip was only interested in getting through this year. He would be retiring next year and the whole office knew he was just treading water now. He seemed to be lost in himself. Everyone else had goals and plans for the coming year. He was preoccupied as usual.

Jon wasn't sure he would like to have that position. It seemed to carry a lot of responsibility and not much recognition. Jon liked recognition. Adele closed the meeting with her pre-canned "let's get to work." She excused herself and exited the room ahead of everyone else.

Jon needed a smoke, so he headed out to the parking lot. Under the lone large oak tree was a small picnic table, put there with smokers in mind. The oak gave a little needed shade, but leaves falling from the branches left messy remains on the table and manicured lawn. The flowers and shrubs on the islands between parking spaces were still colorful; the azaleas were in bloom with shades of red and deep pink. The birds were beginning to be a bit more plentiful.

Jon pulled out his phone and punched in a number.

"Sarasota Sheriff's office, Media desk, this is Lisa Richards."

"Hi Lisa, Jon here," he responded. "How are you? Staying busy?"

"Yeah, pretty busy. What can I do for you?" she answered.

"Did you give it anymore thought, the idea of a series on cold cases? I need something to start with."

"I'm on it, but I have to run it past Cap. I don't think it will be a problem. If you want me to, I can call you later. Say three or four, is that too late?"

"That's okay. I'm meeting Cole for a drink later," Jon came back; never shy in asking for info, he continued. "Say, I have an idea, why don't you join us. We are meeting at Big Bart's on 41. It'll give you a chance to meet Cole and see how the other half lives."

"Thanks for the offer, I'll keep it in mind, maybe another time. But I will call you. I have to go. Talk to you later. Bye." And she was gone.

Jon made a few more notes, stubbed out his cigarette and headed back inside.

Using Google, he pulled up the latest cold cases and printed them off. He studied them trying to visualize any cases that might have potential, something not too old, and something that he would make sensational, something with a backbone, a little mystery and intrigue. Maybe that was stretching it a bit. There were two cases, both about five years old that looked like possibilities. Also, one that was slightly older but might have more appeal; the victim was a local business man. Jon put all the information in his briefcase to see if Lisa could offer something more on each one of these.

*   *   *   *   *

Lisa picked up her note pad and walked towards the captain's office. Tapping lightly on the door, she smiled as he waved her in.

"Quiet today," Cap said motioning her to sit. On one wall were pictures of his predecessors going back to the early 1900's. On the wall directly behind him was his own collection of diplomas and certifications. The small filing cabinet was the resting place for family photos, pictures of his kids growing up.

"Yeah, nothing wrong with quiet. I have a couple things to run past you, if you've got a minute," Lisa crossed her legs and her short skirt slid up on her thigh a bit. Cap didn't miss it, but it took his mind in a direction he swore he wouldn't go.

"Shoot," he said and laughed, bringing his eyes back to meet hers.

"You know I'm putting those public info meetings together and I'm almost done with them. Jon Albee at the Sentinel is running them in the paper for us. He's good about things like that." Lisa paused to make sure Cap was listening to her and not checking out her legs. Although she was afraid he could do both things at once.

"Jon wants to do a series on our cold cases. He needs our help."

"I don't see anything wrong with that. You know Jon, it's all about him. You know what is public and what isn't. Share only what you can." Cap knew most of their publicity wasn't the good kind and he flinched remembering. This was the day and age of throwing stones and apologizing later.

"Do you have any cases in mind? How are you going to do this?"

"I'll probably offer him several names, a few details and let him decide. Then feed him what I can. How does that sound to you?" She knew they had several cold cases and this might help. She also knew cold cases were a problem. They were cold for a reason and the department had been unsuccessful in its petitioning for an actual cold case department. That would mean additional employees and increased funding, a hard sell in these times.

"I don't see a problem now, but ask me later, after he's run the article," he grinned.

The phone on his desk rang and it seemed like a good exit cue for her. "Thanks Cap. I'll keep you informed." She walked out of the office, his eyes on her all the way as he picked up his phone.

Willa saw Lisa enter Cap's office and was watching as she left. She saw the thumbs up as she returned to her desk and hoped this was a good idea. She knew Lisa well enough to know she would get a good spin out of it from Jon, if possible.

Later in the day, Lisa made the call to Jon. They set a date for tomorrow; that would give her time to pull some files and prepare the list of cases that had potential for solving. The more she thought about it the more she liked the idea. She had a thought; Jon would like what she had to offer. She could use him to help fortify their case for adding a much-needed new department; providing his stories were good enough; and she had to admit, he was good at his job.

Barbara Marvin

Chapter 4

Willa opened her eyes, the noise outside was familiar, slipping out of bed, she looked out her window. The waves crashed on the snow-white beach like thunder rolling through the dark sky. She felt awash with gratitude at a day all her own in a place she called paradise and home.

This beach house on Siesta Key had been more than salvation for her. She moved here during one of the lowest points in her life. It restored some normalcy to a life out of control. The house was small having been built in the eighties, but it was perfect for her. Two bedrooms upstairs, the one facing east had become her office; the other facing west looked out over the gulf, allowing her to begin her mornings without the brilliant sun awakening her. Beach life had become music to her ears. The surf rocked her to sleep each night; gently, rhythmically or surging, bellowing as today. Then awakened her each morn.

Despite the wind, with coffee in hand, she walked out on the open veranda. Here there was no denying you were near the gulf. The strong winds from last night had blown the stark white sand on the stone tiles and brightly colored seats. She shook out the cushions and sat down, gazing westward over the rolling waves. The usual population of beach walkers was non-existent; most waiting until the sun was up and shining, except for Otto, a retired old gent from Michigan.

He gave her 'thumbs up', indicating he had already had a little luck today with his metal detector. He appeared several mornings a week searching the beautiful white sand for lost treasures. Occasionally he ambled up and spoke to her. After the first time she met him, she knew his name and had his complete resume. He enjoyed talking almost as much as he enjoyed treasure hunting. He knew she was a detective and said she was the prettiest one he had ever met. By the time the sky was light out he would be long gone. She knew he then went for coffee at

McDonalds to chat with a group of friends who started their day that way.

Finishing her coffee, she left the veranda and hoped for a relaxing day off.

* * * * * *

Lisa and Jon had agreed to meet this morning at a small diner on US 41. It wasn't far from either office, but it would still provide privacy from prying eyes; they felt comfortable here. Lisa had a list of cold cases to share. Jon had gotten here before her and was smiling as she sat down.

"Jon, good to see you," she greeted him openly. He was a good-looking guy, in a way. Too arrogant for her, but then... She wondered why she never saw him with any local women. Maybe they just didn't run in the same social circles.

"You're looking fine yourself," his grin only broadened. Lisa had worn a light sweater over her silky white blouse and dark blue skirt that was short enough to show off her tanned legs. She always wore high heels as they added a couple inches to her height.

This diner had withstood the ages. It was older than Lisa and Jon put together. The décor had changed over the years, whether accidentally or on purpose, it was hard to say. A black counter with chrome seats allowed patrons to eat alone or in large booths that would easily seat six. The high backs on the booths also allowed some coveted privacy. The name had changed a few times; now known simply as Café 41.

Their timing was perfect, as the morning rush was over, and lunch had not begun. There were very few customers, and the ones here were loitering over coffee and reading the paper, which Jon always noticed. The waitress appeared as Lisa sat, a coffee pot in hand. Her name tag said Sally. Lisa thought Sally and the place were about the same age. "Coffee?" Sally asked.

Jon flipped his cup right side up to indicate he needed some and as Sally poured, Lisa did the same. "Could I have one of those chocolate covered donuts?" Lisa asked, pointing to the glass covered cake stand on the end of the counter.

Sally looked at Jon, not saying a word. "Yeah, okay. I'll have a plain one," he replied, shaking his head and laughing. "This is the only place I eat donuts, you cops and your donuts, now I'll have to jog all the way back to the office."

Lisa grinned, "It's not the donuts, it's the sugar! Gets me going! Relax, you'll work it off."

"Now that that business is settled, let's get down to some fun." Jon opened his note book on the table. "I'll show you mine if you'll show me yours?" His grin was expected. He enjoyed his little innuendos; they never bothered Lisa. She just smiled and shook her head.

The one thing she did like about Jon, as opposed to several other local journalists, was his sense of humor and his enthusiasm. He had a way with words whether needing a favor or creating a story for the paper. She put her papers in front of him and he pushed his notes to her side of the table. "Here are a few cases I was able to pull off the internet," he offered.

She compared them to the ones she had written down. "Well, look at these," she said. These were unsolved cases, if they played it right, they might produce renewed interest. That was her objective and that was the direction she would lead Jon. She thought this might just be what it would take to convince local authorities of the need for a budget increase.

Jon was silent as he scanned her notes. "Good. I'm planning a series. I'll focus on one at a time."

"That's fine. But, you know I can only give you things already made public."

"Yeah, I get it," he said, already anticipating how he would extract more from her than she expected to give. Both were quiet for a minute. Sally returned with the donuts and more coffee.

"And," Lisa continued. "I expect positive stories. Give the department credit for something, no bashing. I mean it, Jon. Cap is already walking on eggs, the department, especially Cap, are up for serious review by the higher echelon. This is your chance to start a working partnership with the department. Don't screw it up."

Jon knew how to keep contacts. He had a rule; if he had to print something negative he followed it with something positive to offset it when possible. While other journalists were all about being sensational, Jon knew networking was important for future stories. So, he tried not to burn bridges when writing stories. It usually worked; he would definitely keep that in mind. "Tell me what you need me to say, you know I'll do what I can," he offered.

"Well... glad you have that attitude. I need a favor." Jon, taking notes, was deep in thought as Lisa continued. She could tell he was into this. Time was a precious commodity to her as well as to him, so they wrapped it up.

"Well, I have to get back to the office. Let's meet here in a couple of days." she added as she stood up.

"Ok, and I'll do what I can." He carefully stuffed everything in his briefcase and picked up the tab. Smiling he added, "Thanks, see you in the newspapers."

Lisa laughed. "Okay, Charles!" she replied, recognizing his take on Charles Osgood's closing line as anchor of Sunday Morning News.

*   *   *   *   *

Deadlines were not a problem for Jon, at least not today. Everything had fallen into place for a change. It had been a productive day. He had avoided his boss, Skip, and smiled to himself when he realized it.

He left the office and pulled out into the heavy traffic the season always created. Traveling south on US 41, he knew he wouldn't have to deal with snowbirds long. He pulled into the parking lot at Big Bart's. Big Bart's looked a lot more run down in the glare of the late afternoon sun, because it was. It had been around forever, several different owners, but the bar itself had remained the same.

Anything goes in Bart's, as long as Bart himself was in a good mood. It catered to locals and had no tolerance for anyone else. Jon's friendship with Cole had won Big Bart over; although he was always on probation. Rumor had it that Bart, at 6'4" and nearly 300 pounds had grown up here, served time in local jails for many different offenses, and still managed to maintain his liquor license. Someday, maybe he would write a story about these locals; they sure were an interesting bunch. On second thought, maybe not.

It was dark inside; the only light was from the bar and the pool table. Bart was breaking in a new bartender; the young man could have been a body builder, wide shoulders, narrow hips. He had hands like vise grips and his blonde hair was clipped close to his scalp. He wasn't handsome, but he was interesting. Blue eyes cut right through you and his nose was a bit crooked. It was easy to tell he wasn't local. Jon stood there letting his eyes become accustom to his surroundings. "Hey Jon," Bart boomed.

"Big Bart, how's it going?" Jon drawled. He liked this atmosphere. It was a place where you never used the word décor and Big Bart's in the same sentence if you were trying to morph into a local.

"Good to see you, where's your sidekick, Cole?"

"He's on his way; we've got business tonight," Jon added.

"Yeah?" Bart raised his bushy eyebrows. "Cole writing another expose?"

"You know what he writes is fiction," Jon chided.

"Huh, you could have fooled me. He seems to get pretty damn close to the truth."

Jon stared at Bart. "What's that mean?"

Bart looked up and pointed, "Speak of the devil. Hey Cole, over here."

Cole's eyes adjusted to the room as he headed toward Jon. Scanning the room, he said. "Jon, my old friend, how are you?"

"Fine, you?"

"Where's Bart? Who's that working the bar? I need a drink."

"He left when he saw you coming," Jon teased. "The bartender is new. I think his name is Leif."

"Leaf?"

"Yeah, what are you drinking? Sit down I'll get it." Jon walked to the battered oak bar and ordered two beers.

Jon and Cole had become good friends over the years. Jon had lived here several years. Cole had been born here and would probably die here. He had worked numerous jobs, and nothing satisfied him. One day after meeting Jon and spending many hours in here, he decided to write a book. Fiction, of course. Cole was a story teller from the start. He was a big fan of mysteries and a believer that if you listen long enough, you would have a story to tell. In the scheme of life, it seemed fiction was much more exciting than fact, and it would sell. Cole had transformed himself into what he imagined a writer would be. He let his dark hair grow long, pulling it back with a rubber band, and seldom shaved. Jon had offered to help Cole, since he felt superior and more educated, mentoring would be his contribution.

Barbara Marvin

Chapter 5

Big Bart's was a marathon of beers and brawls. Between the loud cheers and the louder swearing at the pool table, it was anything but quiet in here. Jon learned the bartender's real name was not Leif but Lars. Well it was close enough, he thought.

Jon really enjoyed the stories Cole repeated and it didn't matter if he believed them or not; Cole did. Jon often wondered how Cole could concentrate to write in here. But, hey, that was Cole. He was a moody guy, loved drinking, usually alone and not much else, unless it was happening on a boat. Cole's boat wasn't large, only about fourteen feet long, but he could be found in it, day or night; if he wasn't writing at Big Bart's.

Tonight no one paid them any attention. Cole had become a fixture here. As a matter of fact, he had his own table in the back where he set up his lap top, conducted interviews, and sometimes just pounded out stories. He liked to consider himself the Ernest Hemingway of Sarasota. His favorite Hemingway quote was 'all things truly wicked start from innocence'. He had even visited Key West once; stopping at Sloppy Joe's, a bar famous for allowing Hemingway to write there. He fretted over the fact that no one here got the resemblance, but then, he was sure no one in this bar read much. The amount of drinking Cole did here would probably pay for a real office somewhere else. But, that was another story. He felt indebted to Big Bart for the generosity he showed letting him hang out here so often.

"Ok Cole, give me something to write about," Jon stated. "I'm doing a series on local authors and I'm starting with you. What don't I know about you?" Jon looked him in the eye and leaned in closely. "What makes you tic? What inspires you? What would you like the public to know about you? Or what don't you want them to know?" Jon grinned at him.

Cole looked back, screwed his face up and said. "Well, how about this, I received a death threat yesterday!"

"What!" Jon took a sip of his brew. "Don't bullshit me! I need to write something true... well, as true as you can be," and he laughed.

Cole was studying Jon. Contemplating. Tell him or not?

"What inspired you to write the first novel?" Jon asked before Cole could say a word. "Something I can put in the paper," he added.

"Well you know me, always full of stories. I decided to put it all on paper last year. I sat in this very bar and listened to all the wild tales from some very colorful patrons that shall remain nameless," he glanced around the room. "I jotted down a few lines at first and then decided to expound and exaggerate," he paused. "How does that sound?"

"Good, good, what else?" Jon was taking notes and eyed Cole again. "What else?"

"These guys are so full of it, I couldn't tell fact from fiction… so, I used it all. It made for a pretty good story. One that had a beginning, middle and end," he paused for effect. "So here I am. Waiting to become famous, waiting to become a household name."

They continued to drink and talk. As far as Jon was concerned, Cole was a colorful local and was good entertainment. Earnest Hemingway he wasn't. But there was hope. "Ok, I can fly with what I have. I'll use the picture on the cover of your book, if it's ok with you," Jon said, feeling like he would need a designated driver if he didn't wrap this up soon.

"Yeah, whatever," Cole was just about through for the night, too. They paid the tab and walked out to the parking lot.

"Can you make it home?" Jon asked, wondering if Cole was fit to drive. The last half hour Cole had become moody and totally into himself, hard to converse with and even harder to get a straight answer from. Luckily, he only lived a couple blocks from here, Jon was pretty sure Cole would make it home okay, he only hoped he was right.

"See you later. Call me if we missed anything," Cole directed him as he headed for his truck.

"Ok, I have to put it together, but I think I'm good to go. See ya!"

*   *   *   *   *

Jon could kick himself for drinking so much. He had a deadline looming and found it difficult to close his eyes. He knew he had to hit the road running with this story. And there were many others to follow, providing the first one attracted the needed interest. He liked Cole and hoped this would jump start his writing career. Right now, he was worried about his own career and the direction the local paper was heading. There were plenty of failing newspapers out there. He was aware of the shrinking market for the written word. The cost of a newspaper had gone up just to cover operating cost. The Sentinel covered local news first, local advertising, and with smaller profit margins they had managed to stay afloat. He was thankful for that.

Maybe he would consider a career change; maybe write a book. Tossing his extra pillow over the side of his bed he finally slept.

*   *   *   *   *

Sometimes taking a day off just adds to the workload on your desk the next day; Willa had a lot of paperwork to catch up on and was working at her computer. Her day off had been just that – a day to add more to her workload. At least there was nothing new or exciting on the schedule. Today Russ was off, so she hoped it would be quiet.

"Hey Lisa," she said, looking up for a minute. "How did it go with Jon yesterday? Can he use anything you gave him?"

"Oh yes, you know Jon. As soon as I gave him the list he was formulating a story. He was so wrapped up in his own strategies he even paid for my coffee. That was a first," Lisa laughed. "I'll remember that for the next time."

"When will it hit the paper?"

"Soon. I'm not sure exactly, but it won't be long. He is starting a series; one cold case at a time. He seemed enthusiastic."

"Don't think we'll need to set up a hotline for the response, but tell June on the switchboard, just in case," Willa reminded her.

* * * * *

In the office early, Jon pulled out his notes. He could get in about an hour of hard writing before the daily morning meeting with his boss. Besides his articles about local writers he needed to create an interest in cold cases in this area. He had promised Lisa he could.

His first cold case was a local business man. Jefferson Whitman was killed seven years ago at age 57. He wasn't a large man, stood 5'9" in his bare feet. He was found in his garage just weeks before Christmas. His throat had been cut and his blood had formed a pool around him near his Audi. No signs of a struggle, no broken locks, nothing appeared out of place in the home. Nothing appeared to be missing. Later it was learned one antique pistol was missing. These facts suggested he knew his killer and let him in.

While his home was surrounded by neighbors, the homes were on large wooded lots that provided seclusion and privacy. No one heard or saw anything. Therefore, he was not reported missing for three days.

Jon began to write as he reviewed the entire file. Whitman, a successful banker at the time, had been recently divorced. His ex-wife who had moved to Boston before his death, had inherited everything as he had no heirs. After an investigation, she was moved to the bottom of the suspect list and in the ensuing years nothing had moved her up.

There was a business partner in a real estate operation he was involved in; he was also moved to the bottom of the list. He had no reason to want Whitman dead. Nor did he profit from his death. Quite the contrary, he struggled for a while until the economy finally improved enough for him to buy out the ex-wife and turn the venture around. No suspicions there. The case would need some new evidence or a totally new slant in looking at it.

Staring at his first draft, he decided to write this like a "who done it". If he could come up with enough possible motives and narrative maybe, just maybe someone's memory would be tapped. He readied himself for the meeting with his boss, Skip Davidson.

"Good morning, Skip," Jon said sitting down across from him at the conference table in the small meeting room. Skip looked a little better today than in past days. This room was not much bigger than a large closet; it had a table surrounded by four chairs and a window that overlooked the parking lot.

"Good morning, Jon," Skip answered. "What's happening? How are your stories coming along?"

"I'm working on that cold case series from the sheriff's office. The first one is going to be about Jefferson Whitman. You have any ideas? You were around when Whitman was killed. What was the local gossip, what didn't make the papers?"

"Well, locally, most people thought he had Mafia connections. He made a lot of trips to Chicago," he paused and stared at the water stained ceiling. "And he wasn't as squeaky clean as he appeared."

"Oh? What do you mean?"

"Nothing, that actually got him arrested, but him seemed to be involved in some questionable transactions. He had no obvious enemies; except maybe his ex-wife." Skip added.

"Yeah, but she was practically ruled out. And they were divorced then. They didn't find any female friends, I mean close female friends."

Skip grinned at him like he was delusional. "No female friends, that's a laugh," he said.

"What do you know? Or are you just assuming?" Jon asked, as he perked up. Maybe that would be the twist he needed. Add a little sex and everybody was interested.

"Oh, nothing," Skip replied. "What about your friend Cole, I hear he's got an interview on TV tonight?"

"Oh, Cole, yeah, well I'm doing a spot on him in the paper also. He needs the publicity. His book isn't bad. And I like him. Besides, he's local with lots of local background; this is a local newspaper, if I remember right," Jon was thinking about yesterday's big meeting.

"He has a book signing at the local book store. He's going to talk about growing up here and about his book. I'll be catching it, want to go?" Being as Jon knew Skip would decline, he thought it wouldn't hurt to ask.

After another half hour, they were through with the meeting and Jon was relieved. Skip hadn't been able to add any real information about Whitman, but it gave Jon another angle to pursue.

He needed a cigarette and another cup of coffee. The table in the parking lot was too hot for a very long smoke. The undeniable asset of Florida, the thing that attracted so many tourists, was the lack of a prolonged cool season. It could go from winter to summer in the blink of an eye. The sun was hot today and there had been no rain for a couple days. Jon stubbed out his butt as his phone rang.

"Hello" he saw it was Cole, he looked at his watch, way too early for that guy.

"Hey, Jon old buddy, what's happening?" Cole said.

"Cole, you're up early; new girlfriend kick you out? What can I do for you?"

"You know I don't have a girlfriend. I'm up early on my own. I need coffee... or something. Want to join me?"

"Sorry, can't make it," Jon glanced around. "I've got too much on my plate this morning. Some of us have to work for a living. Some other time."

"Well, okay, sorry I bothered you." His voice sounded a bit off.

"What if I let you buy me a beer tonight?" Jon quickly added.

"Okay, I can do that, see ya then. Bye," and Cole hung up. Jon looked at his phone, puzzled. He wondered what was really on Cole's mind. Well it would have to wait until tonight.

The heat radiating off the parking lot was enough for Jon to renew his resolution to stop smoking. Almost. Leaving the smoking area, he searched his phone for the number of his next interview. Sarah Jones was next on his list of local authors. Since she was free they agreed to meet in one hour. Just enough time for him to skim her book and prepare a list of questions for her, in case she needed prompting. Her book was a visitor's guide to local known and unknown points of interest.

Jon's day went as planned; his interview with Sarah went well. He wrote an interesting story about her life and her interests in Florida. She had visited some pretty strange places and had written about them well. She had a great sense of humor and it came across in her guide. There were old Indian burial grounds, the first home of the Ringling Brothers, what used to be the celery fields of Sarasota; and the renown locations of several Florida murders. Her book would be the perfect segue from Cole's. She wasn't bad looking, either. Old enough to be Jon's mother, but she had a busy social life and included those places that were interesting to visit purely for social activities.

Back in the office, Jon lined up several other local authors that looked interesting. There were more to choose from than he first imagined. This was great, he thought, because it would allow him to be more selective.

After a busy working day, Jon closed his desk and computer and headed south. He made a mental note to go easy on the beer tonight; last night he imbibed a little too much. Cole's TV interview would air tonight, and he was sure Big Bart would have it on; so he would be there.

Cole seemed like his old self; jeans and a Florida Gator's tee shirt, his usual attire, no mention of this morning's early call. Both men seemed to be going slow on the drinking. They drank and watched the interview. Cole was a star here, even though he was trying to act like this happened every day, no big deal. Everyone was whooping and hollering, patting him on the back, and giving high five's. Lots of free booze.

Jon rated the interview a six, maybe. Not great, but the local newsman did a good job of keeping Cole on point. Luckily, it was not live, and they easily bleeped out the unacceptable words Cole had used.

After the other patrons returned to their usual drinking, pool playing, and dart throwing, things were a little quieter. Cole's moodiness returned, and he complained of being tired. "What do you say, we call it a day?" he suggested.

"Okay... I know you have a busy day tomorrow with the book signing," Jon offered. Cole just nodded. In the parking lot Cole glanced around; then got in his truck as Jon waved to him.

Cole would be fine tomorrow, Jon thought.

Barbara Marvin

Chapter 6

This day felt different; although it had begun the same as all other days. Luther hesitated as he pushed open the big door with its bright red and yellow trim. Today he noticed just how heavy it was. Taking a deep breath, the aroma of freshly brewed coffee filled his nostrils. He glanced to his right at a table in the rear and waved. There were his coffee-drinking friends, already highly animated in conversation.

Luther's daily routine didn't deviate much from day to day; the sun rose, the sun set, he couldn't complain, life was good. He had been an investment broker for many years before he retired. Following his own advice for his portfolio; he was living the life many retirees only dreamed of. It had been a stressful life before he left his job and the high-powered goals and ambitions. It made him appreciate his retirement even more, but at that moment boring quickly came to mind as he reminisced about the past.

With coffee in hand, he smiled as he approached the table where he would begin his last day on Earth. If he had only known.

There was George, a retired detective who sometimes walked with a cane. He had a big mouth, but he wasn't the only one. His short haircut was a holdover from his days on the local force. His son was also a detective, who never quite measured up to his dad. Sometimes his son redeemed himself by calling and letting his dad in on something exciting happening in the office. George then regaled in relaying these pearls of information to his friends over coffee. It made him feel connected, like he still had it. He was married, and his wife did her best to keep him busy in the community. They delivered meals to shut-ins and volunteered at the local Senior Center. Occasionally, when the wife was sick he roped Luther into helping him. Of course, that caused Luther to alter his daily routine.

And Otto was a retired accountant for Ford Motors in Michigan. He thought it was a good thing that Luther drove a Ford F-150 and wished everyone did because he thought that's what kept his retirement fund going. He usually left the restaurant with a pocketful of sugar packets. No need to buy them when he could get them for free, a behavior that embarrassed Luther. He never had to buy straws or napkins either. He was on the beach before sunup most days searching for treasures, using his metal detector like a holy grail. Each item found was documented along with conjured up stories of what could have happened. His journal was full of exciting things, all the products of his imagination. Give him a pen and he would give you an adventure. One day, he said, he was going to write a book. Maybe he would. He was a widower and seemed to have plenty of time on his hands. The unknown was fascinating to him.

Last, but definitely not least, was Tom. Also retired but still dabbling in his company real estate business from time to time. He had been married several times, but who's counting. Right now, he was single and quite handsome, even at 70. His gray hair styled like a model out of GQ magazine. He could spot a single woman a mile away, he boasted. He spent many nights at the local watering hole and sometimes came away lucky. When he did, they all knew about it. Sarasota had its share of attractive widows looking for a good time. His medicine cabinet was well stocked with Viagra and he made no excuses for his desire to use it. Luther expected him to have notches on his bedpost and wondered how much of what he shared was true and how much was the product of wishful thinking and an overactive imagination.

Luther, still smiling said, "Hey guys, you're early."

"You're late," they said in unison. Although he knew he wasn't.

"What's with you? Can't get out of bed? Or did you finally find a date?" Tom ragged on him.

"I'm just moving slow, I guess, no date," he replied thinking he should tell Tom he had a date just to see the look on his face.

"What's new since yesterday?" Otto asked looking at Luther.

"I'm going fishing today. How about joining me? I found the perfect place for snapper and snook," he replied.

"No, not today for me. How about the rest of you bums?" Otto answered shaking his head. "Where is this great place? Maybe I'll get over there someday."

"It's just south of my slip, on the same side of the bay; about a mile down. There are some pilings sticking out, I think it was an old dock that bit the dust. But it creates some shade and the water is deep. I'm going late, just before dark, if you change your mind let me know."

"Hey, let me tell you about this woman I met last night," Tom changed the subject. "I think she is the one!"

All three men looked at Tom and roared.

"Yeah, like we've never heard that before!"

Tom laughed, too and said, "I didn't mean to … you know … settle down with."

"Well, now that we got that straight, I feel better," George said pretending to wipe sweat from his brow. "Did you watch the news last night? That was some major wreck on the interstate. People drive way too fast anymore."

"Yeah, that's why I don't drive my truck far," Luther interjected. "I go to the grocery store, I go to the dock, and I come here. That's it for me. Look out there on 41, right now. It's stop and go." All eyes turned toward the highway where traffic was already a nightmare; the sun dancing off each rooftop like sparklers on the Fourth of July. They were quiet for a moment.

This group formed several years ago. None of them could remember the exact time they met or the reason. It didn't matter; what mattered was that they got along well together. As diverse as they were, they always managed to have a few laughs.

Luther's eyes scanned the room; it looked like it did every other day. There were young kids on their way to school, men and women on their way to work, and then us, the old geezers. The only ones not in a hurry. After several hours of loud and opinionated versions of worldly affairs and raunchy sexual tidbits, usually from Tom, they were ready to go their separate ways.

In the parking lot, the heat was shimmering off the cars and the noise level from the road had reached an agonizing level. Luther pulled his truck out of the lot into westbound traffic without incident, staying in the right lane. He was home in less than ten minutes. Pulling off Stickney Point Road into his driveway gave him a feeling of comfort. Home.

He parked his truck precisely in the middle of the carport, exactly 10 feet from the door. He was not compulsive but some things he liked a certain way. Like his tool shed, if anyone looked in they would swear he had OCD. Everything was in its space; tools were outlined on the pegboard, each in the correct spot. Fishing gear was arranged on a shelf by size in descending order. All rags hung on hooks and the place was spotless.

He mowed his own lawn and had created a haven for relaxing under a small oak tree. There he had placed a small metal table with four uncomfortable outdoor chairs. It looked nice, but he usually brought a canvas back chair to sit in when he came out to read. He never left the chair out when he went in. He folded it and placed it neatly in the shed before he went inside. The few shrubs were neatly trimmed. He liked seeing things grow; his wife would have liked it too. He had a few things to do before he went fishing and he didn't want to start thinking about Helen. He knew he would just sit and feel sorry for himself and that was unacceptable.

He had taken an early retirement to be with Helen in her final days. They had planned to move to Florida, together. After she passed away, he couldn't make the move; it felt like betrayal. Like adultery. It took his kids three years before they convinced him to move on with his life.

He came to Sarasota one year with his son to go fishing and that's when he decided to cut the cord, quit moping, and get on with his life. He hadn't been sorry, but at times he still missed talking to her. Living alone had it ups and downs. Fishing had become a tonic for him. He needed it when he was restless or if he was too relaxed. He just needed to fish. He bought a small boat, docked it in a rented slip and was living out his preprogrammed life; just the way his kids had engineered it.

It was late afternoon when he finished his chores and left to go fishing. Traffic was heavy; the sun was low, shining in his eyes, but he wouldn't need his glasses for very long. The dock was less than a mile, but he didn't hurry. The later the better as he expected to be out after dark,

He parked in his usual place, collected his gear and bag from the bed of his truck and walked to his slip. When he stepped on the boat a tranquil belonging touched him. He always felt this calmness, serenity, and belonging wash over him here. Loading his gear into the boat he glanced around, surprised to see he was alone at the dock. He didn't mind ... sometimes the small talk with other fishermen was more than he wanted to deal with. Today was one of those days.

He cranked up the boat and move out at a fast clip, holding his khaki fishing hat to keep it from blowing off his head. He headed south, knowing where there were several abandoned and broken docks. Good place to catch his limit tonight.

When the area came into sight he shut off the motor. He drifted a little until he was almost under the few standing pilings. He got lucky. It didn't take him long to catch more than he could eat. By now the sun was setting fast. He loved this time of day. Great time to fish; even better time to enjoy the peace and quiet. He had done this many times and never tired of it.

The seagulls were loud, diving at him in hopes of stealing the treats he always brought for them. He tried counting them as they swooped down, but they were too fast for him. They stayed around long enough to finish off the crackers. He watched as they flew away into the darkening sky. Pelicans were flying low and in formation heading to their own final destination for the night.

After the sun set, it wouldn't take long for the blues and reds and golds to become dark overhead. Today had been a day full of memories; and tonight, those thoughts were still winding in his mind, tugging at forgotten tidbits of happiness. He closed his eyes. Maybe he could drift out to sea; leave this world and be with Helen. He didn't remember how long his mind was deep in another time and place with memories of happier times when he thought he heard voices. He opened his eyes. The sound was muted and coming from across the bay; he tried to focus on what was happening. It was hard to see in the darkening evening; the three men outlined against the light from the large stucco house seemed to be struggling with a large bundle.

They talked very little and managed to position a parcel in the bottom of the boat. He could hear what sounded like a chain clinking and he stared at the activity. What were they doing? His first thought was illegal drugs. Drugs were a very big issue in the south, with boats bringing them in from South America, Mexico, and other places.

He reached for his bag, opened it quietly, and removed his binoculars. Careful not to make a sound. What he saw confused him even more. He didn't know what drug trafficking looked like, maybe this was it, but it didn't look at all like what he had expected. The bundle, which appeared to be wrapped in blue plastic was about 5 or 6 feet long and not very big around.

He continued to watch. The old adage 'curiosity killed the cat' sprung to his mind.

But still, the binoculars were aimed across the bay. With his left hand, he fumbled in his bag for his phone. Lowering the binoculars and raising the phone, he snapped several pictures. He wasn't sure why, in the fading light, it was unlikely that he could get a clear picture. Then just as quietly he returned the phone and binoculars to his bag and focused on the three men. He had taken pictures with his phone before, but not at night, in the dark. He would check when he got home to see if it was even possible.

It seemed to take the strength of all the men to do whatever they were doing. They glanced around, oblivious to Luther hidden in the semi-darkness in the pilings. As soon as they finished with the chains, the one which seemed to be in charge raised his hand in a gesture, cranked up the motor, and left the dock. Racing off at full speed they were soon out of sight.

Luther felt uneasy; he put away his equipment and felt the urge to get out of there. So, he started his engine and pulled out of his fishing spot. His mind was racing wondering what he had witnessed. He was apprehensive; should he report it. What would he report? He saw three guys putting something heavy in a boat? Had he witnessed a crime or what? Who would he report it to?

Dark, at full speed he kept his eyes straight ahead, almost as if he could un-see whatever it was he saw. He never looked back. Perhaps he should have.

Standing at the shoreline across the bay where the other boat had been, stood a lone shadow. The shadow moved quickly when he saw Luther. Phone in hand, he disappeared.

The few minutes it took Luther to get out of the boat and into his truck were filled with jumbled thoughts causing him to forget to clean his fish, a job he always did at the dock.

Traffic was light on the way home. Maybe he would just wait till the morning; he could tell the guys and see what they thought he should do. George used to be a detective. He would know what to do. With that thought, he heaved a sigh of relief as he turned into his driveway. He parked his car precisely in the middle of the carport and exactly ten feet from the door and relaxed. Routine calmed him. Home calmed him. Thinking of his friends calmed him.

As he opened his truck door and stepped out, his calmness dissipated like late evening showers. A dark SUV had pulled in quickly behind him.

Chapter 7

"Heads up. Body found near 41 South and Stickney Point Road."

Every head recoiled and every eye opened wide, as the dispatcher's voice came in loud and clear, continuing with the exact location not far from Willa's home.

"Let's go Kevin," Willa said as she kicked back her chair and grabbed her jacket. Kevin was riding with her. Why does this have to happen now, she thought? Russ off and I'm stuck with Kevin.

"Okay, I'll drive," he answered half out the door. One thing about Kevin, he was always ready.

The county issued vehicle hit Morrell Street and made a left turn. US 301 was awash with sunshine and heavy traffic. Kevin swore at the drivers reacting so slowly to his flashing blue lights, but Willa was grappling with her own demons, mental images. Just last year a day like today had turned her life upside down. It had turned the town upside down. Her mind was playing tricks on her; she was seeing a body, a body wrapped from head to toe in surgical gauze. The throat sliced clean, a body that wasn't just a body. It was the remains of her ex-husband. She shook her head, trying to erase those pictures as US 301 merged with US 41.

"What?" Kevin glanced at her out of the corner of his eyes.

"Nothing... just drive."

Traffic moved to the right allowing them access. Kevin was a good driver, but at this speed, Willa felt the need to brace herself on the dash. "Hey, take it easy," she cautioned him.

"Sorry," he moaned, "I know that area; my Dad lives near there, in that mobile home park on the other side of Stickney. I'll bet anything, he's already there."

"Well, it will be your job to contain him! Got that?" Willa wanted him to be on his toes, and she was concerned because Russell was off today. She was stuck with Kevin. His dad could be a pain in the ass; a retired detective, living out his retirement in a socially active community. He felt it was his right to keep up with anything happening in the county, expecting his son to keep him in the loop. Knowing what she did about Kevin, she hoped she could keep from killing him today. Boy, she missed Russell. She wasn't happy as they turned right onto Stickney Point Road. They could see the action from here.

Kevin braked hard on the shell drive. The small mobile home looked well-kept, but the yard was now a parking lot for a wide variety of emergency vehicles, red and blue lights were flashing as if in sync.

The fire department had been first on the scene with an EMT truck and another ambulance. There were patrol cars and several other vehicles already on the job. Kevin parked the department Ford east of everyone else. "This looks big," he said.

Willa grabbed her bag as she jumped from the vehicle and eyed the ever-growing crowd behind the yellow crime scene tape. "Yeah, it does." She was in detective mode as she surveyed the scene, already processing the freshly mown grass and the very clean carport.

One glance made Kevin cringe. There was his father waving to him as he hastened to the front door. Kevin waved back and yelled, "I'll see you in a minute, wait where you are." Turning to Willa, he quietly added "I told you my dad would be here."

She could only roll her eyes as she saw him. One of the men standing with him was a man she recognized. This might help, she thought.

This mobile home was typical of many in the area; except it stood alone on an average size lot surrounded by vacant lots. No close neighbors. The person living here was a fisherman. Several dip nets hung in a row on the outside of the shed along with a very old bait bucket. The shed was locked with a shiny new Yale padlock. The Ford truck had been parked precisely in the middle of the carport, but the driver's door was open.

Willa glanced in the bed of the truck; two fishing rods were wedged against the cab, held in place by a cooler, a bait bucket, and a small toolbox. Near the tailgate was a galvanized bucket with several fish. Seeing the truck door open and the unclean fish suggested the driver had been approached immediately after parking. After using her phone to take several pictures they approached the door. Now to take a look inside.

The smell of death was strong; it hit you like a slap in the face. The coppery bite stung your nostrils and conjured up images of what they were about to see. "I'm Detective Vasser. This is Detective Dupree." Kevin said to the patrolman standing there. "What happened here?"

"Thanks for getting here so fast. I'm Patrolman Roger Sinclair." he said holding his hand over his mouth and nose. "This smell is killing me. How do you guys stand it?" he paused. "Those men standing there," he said pointing to a group of men behind the yellow tape, "found their friend dead a short time ago. It seems they usually congregate at McDonald's every morning."

Willa and Kevin glanced at the men; they all appeared to be in their 70's or 80's. Tee shirts, shorts, and Crocs was the uniform of the day. Two of the men seemed visibly shaken. The other was George Vasser, Kevin's father.

"Okay, we'll get to them. First, let's go inside," Kevin said and motioned for Willa to follow him.

"Sinclair, you can catch your breath in the carport."

"Thanks, I will."

"Sinclair," Willa nodded towards the truck, "was the truck door open or has someone started checking it out?"

"It was like that when I got here. No one has been near it since."

"Thanks. Keep it like that," she ordered.

After donning plastic footies and rubber gloves, they stepped inside. The scene was ghastly. No body was in sight, but blood was everywhere. Chairs were over turned, the table rammed against a wall, and a small plaque had fallen and broken, scattering glass on the table. The plaque showed a fisherman casting his line into the gulf. It said, "Welcome to Paradise". She pointed to the broken plaque, "Yeah, welcome to paradise."

Stale air and a few other unknown smells were competing with the smell of death. Willa gagged, reached inside her pocket for her Vicks and her mask her face damp with perspiration. This was the scene of a struggle. The heat had an obvious influence on what they were seeing and smelling. With the windows closed and the air conditioner off it was probably over 100 degrees inside.

It was clearly the home of an older person, probably a man. Most older women had pictures of children, grandchildren and friends everywhere. Not much personal stuff here. The magazines scattered across the floor were mostly fishing and hunting magazines. After spending time in the room that was apparently the place where the crime had occurred, they moved through a small hallway to the bedroom.

The body in the bedroom was lying on a blood-soaked mattress in a serene, hands folded over his chest, posed position. Interesting, thought Willa. It seemed all the violence had occurred in the front room. The victim had snow white hair and a body now shrunken and wrinkled, probably in his 70's. Who would do this to you? Willa thought. She stared at the man lying in his own bed, posed as if at rest. He was fully clothed, although his shirt was ripped in many places. He had on one rubber boot, the other had been in the living room. He was attacked as he returned from fishing, didn't even have time to change boots. They did not know the time of death, yet. There were multiple wounds to the torso and neck.

What could have caused someone to want to kill you, she thought again, as she stared at the face of this victim. Someone killed you and then took the time and energy to pose your body. Why? She shook her head.

The mobile home was now crowded with technicians and crime scene photographers. Nothing could be moved until all the pictures were taken and evidence gathered.

As more technicians entered the bedroom, Willa and Kevin moved out of the small room, through the small living room, and continued outside to begin interrogations.

Willa removed her mask and took a deep breath. Someone was walking toward them. "Hey Mr. Vasser," Willa said

"Hey Dad," Kevin added.

"Kevin, Willa, good to see you both. This is terrible, just terrible," George was mopping his brow with a large white handkerchief. "I knew Luther; he was a good man. We had coffee together almost every day. You know the old guys group, me and those guys standing there. What a shock."

Kevin looked at his dad, "Really?"

"Yes, that's what I'm telling you."

Willa wasn't surprised to see Mr. Vasser, but she was surprised to hear he was close friends with the deceased. This might be a big break. "Kev, put your dad in the car, I'm going over to talk to the others," Willa nodded towards the other two old guys and walked towards them.

"Hello Otto," she said recognizing him from the beach and addressing the other man, "My name is Detective Dupree, which of you knew Luther?"

"We both do," Otto said, taking the lead as the obvious spokesman for the two. "We had coffee together four or five days a week."

"One at a time, give me your name and address," she had her notepad in her hand and was ready to begin. After statements from each, she glanced over at Kevin, "Please stay here, I'll be right back."

Kevin didn't need help with his dad, which surprised Willa. Under the circumstances George Vasser was very professional. He had explained how the men got together. "When Luther didn't show up, I called him, his phone went right to voice mail. So, we decided to see what the problem was. We saw his truck in the carport and suspected he was sick or overslept. He's done that before."

He paused to make sure everything was being noted. "The smell was the first thing that got to us, after knocking and trying the door. The door was unlocked. Well, you can imagine our reaction. We closed the door and called 9-1-1 and waited for you to show up."

Spectators were drawn like magnets where there was police action. Patrol cars directed traffic and helped keep everyone at bay.

Although the yard was at full capacity, Journalist Jon Albee found a place to park not too far away. He and his camera man headed toward the crowd to start his story. Today was a headliner day. The yellow tape kept him at a distance, right there with the rest of the onlookers.

Jon recognized the detectives as they exited the mobile home. His cameraman was on it. He zoomed in on them as Jon yelled, "Hey Detectives can you give me a word?"

Willa looked up and saw Jon and shook her head. "Not now."

Jon glanced around for a possible interviewee and zoned in on a seventyish looking man. He was alert, tan, and had eyed Jon also. "Excuse me, I'm Jon Albee, Sarasota Sentinel, could you tell me what you saw?"

"Well, I think someone was killed. I know the owner of this place, just can't say if it's him."

Jon continued speaking to this man whose name was Rudy Washington and then moved on to several others; all very willing to speak to a reporter. He remained on the scene after they removed the body. His camera man was able to get some clear pictures of the detectives leaving as they wrapped up their story.

Kevin and Willa stayed on the scene until early afternoon. In that time, they were able to interview the men that discovered his body and learned the names of his next of kin. All Luther's close relatives lived in North Carolina. After the medical examiner released the body to the morgue, they finished up their business and headed back to the office.

It was still a crime scene; so an officer was left to guard against any unauthorized trespassing.

This day, that had started slow and uneventful like so many others, had become very arduous.

Chapter 8

Today Jon was covering Cole's book signing. He would show up and make a big splash about local authors, excite the crowd, if there was one, get a few interviews with customers, snap a couple pictures, and leave him to bask in his glory. Cole could thank him tonight at Big Bart's by buying the beer. It would appear in the paper in two days.

As luck would have it, he finished his story on the homicide in time to focus on Cole's book signing; it was at BAM, Books a Million, at one o'clock.

He grabbed a bite to eat at the deli and checked his wallet, made sure he had cash. Even though he had read the book before it was published, he wanted to support Cole and actually purchase a copy. Maybe he would even buy 2; he could always give one to his cousin, Sarah. She loved mysteries and would be thrilled to get a copy signed by the author. He headed to the mall and parked. Maybe Cole was drawing a crowd. The temperature was hot and sweat rolled down his face. Jon had to admit, he was looking forward to this event. He had his fingers crossed that Cole would make a good impression and sell a few books. The store always did a good job promoting local authors. For Cole it was his first opportunity to sell his book. He had left a few free copies at Big Bart's.

Walking in the front door he could see a crowd gathered in the middle of the store. Wow! Cole had garnered a few people. He strode directly to the busy area, checking out the full-length poster of Cole on the way. It showed a very photographic face; book in hand, crooked smile and all. Several stacks of Cole's book allowed readers easy access. The book itself looked good; Jon had helped design the cover. A Florida beach in the back ground with a view of woods in the foreground and shadowy figures lurking near.

Jon picked up a copy, thumbed through it, expectantly listening for Cole's off the cuff commentary. Customers were talking, perusing their copy of the featured book. The line had formed in front of the table. Customers would pay for their book and then have them personally autographed. Jon glanced through the readers to get a glimpse of the man of the hour.

To his surprise, Cole wasn't seated at the table. No pen in hand. No happy smile. No Cole. He surveyed the room, no sign of Cole. He could hear the customers asking, "Where is the author? I thought he would be here."

"Sorry, he's been delayed," was the answer given.

Jon backed away from the people and pulled out his phone. Pushing through the front door, he hit Cole's number. On the sidewalk, in the heat, he heard the phone ring. "Hey Cole, pick-up... Hey man, where are you?" he said out loud as he listened to the phone ring. He waited till the voice mail came on before admitting Cole wasn't going to answer the phone. Scanning the parking lot for Cole's pickup truck was not successful. He tried again to reach him by phone; no luck.

Jon was beginning to get infuriated with his friend. He turned and reentered the store, pushing his way to the desk; the one so neatly set up with copies of the book, pictures of Cole, and still milling customers hoping to see a real local author.

"Excuse me," he said to the young woman behind the register that had been conveniently placed at the end of the table.

She looked at him and smiled and he knew before he asked that she had no idea what was going on or where Cole had disappeared. "Never mind," he mumbled as he turned and left the building.

Leaving the parking lot Jon drove south, past Big Bart's. A quick glance did not reveal Cole's pickup in the lot. He continued to Cole's apartment complex. The ten apartments were in a single row and Jon's was the first one on the end. There was a covered sidewalk along the front of the building which helped when it was raining. The back entrances had an open slab of concrete, barely big enough to be called a porch. Although the one-story units were in need of paint, a few other major repairs, and probably didn't conform to any regulations, renters were required to park in assigned spaces. Cole's space was right in front of his apartment.

Relieved, Jon saw Cole's 10-year-old rusty gray pickup. Relieved and angry, he pulled into an empty space right beside it and parked. It was an assigned spot, but he didn't plan on being long and visitor parking was not convenient. A dozen excuses were playing out in his mind; the one he expected was, Cole was drunk, again. This had been a big deal for him and he had screwed it up.

Jon rapped loudly on the door. He could hear the TV, but no Cole. He pounded again louder. The front drapes were closed, and he couldn't see in, so he headed around the back. Banging on the kitchen door got the same results. "Cole," he called. "Cole get up!"

Still no answer. He pulled out his phone and punched in Cole's number and listened. Somewhere inside he heard a phone ring, then silence as it went to voice mail. No Cole.

Now Jon was getting worried. Cole wasn't that hard to wake up and he shouldn't be that drunk this early in the day. What now? He walked around to the front and a thought occurred. Jumping back in his car, he headed north and pulled into Big Bart's. Walking in he let his eyes adjust to the lack of light.

"Jon you're drinking mighty early, what will it be?" Big Bart greeted him as he walked in.

"I'm not drinking; I'm looking for Cole, have you seen him?"

"Not since last night," he replied.

"Did he come back after I left."

"No... I think he was talking to a few people earlier, no one in particular. He was drinking, that's all I remember. But if I see him, I'll tell him you are looking for him," Bart said as he continued to wipe the bar.

Jon nodded 'Okay' and walked out in the blaring sun. Shaking his head, he said to himself, "I'm not his baby sitter. I've got to get to work."

Cole had missed a good opportunity and if he expected Jon to help him promote his book, well, he had better have a good excuse for this screw up. But in the back of his mind, Jon was worried.

Barbara Marvin

Chapter 9

Willa and Kevin had worked late into the night but were back at it early. Nothing pumped her more than a hard case, a chance to validate her worth, her reason for being here. Her desire to show she was worth the job she was paid for.

As Russell walked in, after a day off, his look of determination was evident. He was on board, but only Willa knew that.

"Hey Russ, good to see you back! Guess what you missed?" Kevin spouted. Willa cut her eyes to Kevin and then to Russell. Russell smiled back.

"I'm here; let's get started." Russell replied. He had heard the news on the radio on his late return from his Lake Okeechobee fishing trip and called Willa. After he listened to her ragging about being left with Kevin she gave him all the evidence they had so far. She reluctantly admitted Kevin did pretty well at the scene. Maybe he was maturing some and his dad could be an asset. Mr. Vasser was scheduled to come in today along with his friends.

Captain Dunbar stepped out of his office and motioned everyone to join him.

"Good morning, Cap," Willa said.

As Willa, Kevin, Russell, and Frank filed in, Captain Dunbar was already addressing them. Early morning meetings were held in his office. He had set the stage to have all the detectives work together on this. Willa sensed a change in the captain. It wasn't his urgency about this case because he was always on target; today was different.

"Every morning we will meet in this office first, go over any progress and every new lead. This is a department venture. Work together, the white board will be updated as needed. No time off, no sick days. Let's get this solved!"

"Since Russell and Frank were both out yesterday, Willa fill them in, will you?" he ordered, as he made notes in his small note pad and carefully slipped it in his shirt pocket.

"Yesterday a local man, Luther Landrow, was found murdered," she looked at Frank the expert technical support agent. "Frank, hope you had a good few days off because it's going to require all of us on this one."

Referring to her notes she said, "Landrow, age 73, living alone, no known enemies, was murdered in his home. Autopsy isn't in yet. Throat cut, no knife found at the scene. At least none used to do the job. Living room was bloody - walls, floor, couch. It appears to be the room where he was killed. His body was in the bedroom, laid out on the bed, hands folded over his chest in a posed position. Very serene, if you ask me; very staged. We have yet to define the reason for the posed position. It has all the characteristics of a hit." Willa took a breath, nodding to Kevin.

"Yes, the crime scene was odd," he added. "We believe he died the day before his body was discovered. And guess who found him?

My dad, they were friends. They usually met for coffee and when he failed to show up and didn't answer his phone they went to check on him. My dad and his friends found him," he repeated.

The meeting continued until they had covered everything they had. The group left Cap's office and went back to their own desks.

* * * * *

If Jon had time, he would be worried. Was Cole showing his true colors now or was there something terribly wrong? He finished his report and looked at his phone; once again he punched in Cole's number. He couldn't help but remember funny times with Cole, but he had never done something like this before and this wasn't funny. His voice mail was full. Jon knew Cole was never without his phone; this worried him even more.

How long did he have to wait before he could report him missing, twenty-four hours, forty-eight hours? He was an adult; could he even say he was missing? He eyed his phone. This time he punched in a different number.

"Sarasota Sheriff's Office, media desk. This is Lisa, how may I help you?"

"Hi Lisa, Jon here."

Before he could finish, Lisa replied. "Yeah, Jon, sorry I don't have time to chat, call me later if you don't mind."

"Hey Lisa, wait. I need to ask you a couple of questions," he added quickly. "I need to know how long I have to wait before I can file a missing person's report."

"You need what?" she asked.

"How long before I can file a missing person's report?"

"Who's missing?"

"I haven't been able to find Cole; he missed his book signing, his truck is at his apartment, but he's not there. I can't reach him!"

"Okay Jon, the facts are, there is no waiting period legally. It's not like you see on TV. If you know a person is missing you can report it as soon as you feel they are missing. Do you want to make a report?"

"Ummm, yes I do," Jon was hesitant. "Can I come in and talk to someone?"

"Yes, come on in. Someone will take your report," Lisa informed him.

"Thanks Lisa, I'll be over in a few!" Jon hung up. Was this smart? Is he really missing? He was torn between finding his friend and looking like a fool if Cole was just... well, being Cole. The dilemma ate at him until he could sit no longer.

At the sheriff's office the receptionist buzzed him in. "Hi June, good to see you," he said to her.

"Hey Jon, what can I do for you today?" she knew him by name since he was no stranger at their office.

"I need to file a missing person's report." There he said it, practically holding his breath.

"One minute. I'll get an officer for you," she replied.

Willa walked out to meet him. "Jon, how are you? Come in, I'll find us a room," she stated. Jon was unusually quiet as he followed her to conference room two. "Have a seat, what's going on?" she needed to get right to the point as she was very busy.

"Well, I can't find my friend, Cole," he said.

"Okay," she paused. "What do you mean, you can't find Cole?"

Jon was specific on every detail, after all he was a reporter. He wanted Willa to know, he felt something wasn't right. She was very attentive, taking notes and filling out the forms.

"Okay Jon, I will send someone out to check on him," she said.

"What can I do, what if you don't find him?"

Willa eyed him with curiosity. "You think something has happened to him?"

"I don't know... I feel... strange about this. Cole has done some weird things, but still..."

"We will check his apartment for starters; see if there is any sign of an accident. We'll check his truck, check his phone. And we'll get back to you."

"Oh, by the way," Jon added. "he has a boat, maybe he got stranded out in the gulf or something."

"Okay, the Coast Guard can check that." Willa was anxious to wrap this up. After all, most of the time missing adults showed up after a day or two. Usually, they went somewhere on the spur of the moment and didn't think to let anyone else know.

As they stood to leave the room Jon asked, "Detective, do you have any leads on that Stickney Point murder? My article is front page. What can you tell me?"

"Listen, Jon," she stopped and looked him in his eyes. "I hope that's not why you are here! I hope you are really concerned about your friend."

"Yes, I am concerned about Cole… but while I'm here, well I thought I would ask. Thanks a lot for your time. I'll wait to hear from you," he continued out the door as Willa headed to her desk.

She stopped at Lisa's desk. "What do you know about Jon's friend Cole?"

"Not much, never met him. Jon gave me a copy of his book; I'll pass it on to you when I'm finished." Lisa replied.

"Okay," she replied. "Don't know when I'll have time to read it." After writing up the report, Willa contacted patrolman Paul Forrest. He would start at Cole's apartment. She checked with the Coast Guard to see if there had been any reports of boats adrift. She worked rapidly knowing this was a major case staring her in the face.

Barbara Marvin

Chapter 10

Kevin and Russell were at the back of the office, intently scrutinizing the white board. Their conversation was muted. Nothing new had been added and Willa felt this was going to be a rough one. When you have someone murdered for no apparent reason it is especially difficult. Willa felt this was one of those. With a lot of hard work and maybe, some good old-fashioned luck, they might find the answers they needed to solve this case.

Kevin looked up as she approached. "Willa, my dad is on his way over. I'm setting up all three conference rooms for the interviews. His friends are with him; we'll interview them, again. Who do you want? My dad, Otto what's his name or Tom?"

"I'll take Otto; you take Tom and Russell and can deal with your Dad. Is that ok with you?" she asked.

"Yeah, fine! Russell?" now both sets of eyes were focused on Russell.

"Ok by me." Russell said, nodding his head. Russell would be good with the other Vasser; he didn't mince words, didn't walk on eggshells. He was a hard-nosed detective and right now that's what they needed.

Willa was a little surprised by Kevin; he seemed to be taking some initiative. Maybe he was growing up. Why did she always think of him as a kid? Because he was! She knew he was intimidated by his father and she knew how that felt. He needed to prove himself every day. She knew how that felt, too. These were the feelings of inadequacy that had pushed her to become the woman she was; a woman never again to be over shadowed by a man. This also plagued her in every personal relationship she ever attempted. Maybe this would push Kevin to mature into the kind of detective they could count on.

She had a full plate but couldn't help but think about Jon and his friend Cole. She had sent a patrolman to check the apartment, he should be back soon. She pushed that problem to the back of her mind. She had other major problems that warranted her full attention. The first homicide of the year topped the list for major. What had Luther done to bring this upon himself? A quiet man, or so everyone seemed to think. No apparent ties to illegal activities. Was he just in the wrong place at the wrong time? He had been fishing, what else had he been doing just prior to this horrible fate? Someone must have followed him home and... that was the end of Luther, but why?

This would require all the expertise of this office. There was Russell, the detail man, nothing escaped him, and he was easy to work with, a team player. If Kevin's father had anything useful, Russell would find it. Kevin was young and inexperienced, but she could see hope that he was maturing on the job. His personal life was a rat race. He was focused on setting some kind of record with the ladies. However, Russell kept him in line at work.

Frank was support services with a capital S. There was nothing he didn't know about computers and how to access them. He had been around a long time, longer than Captain Dunbar. He was constantly taking new classes and talked about teaching as a second job in the near future. Willa felt close to all these guys.

She looked down at the report on her desk. Luther's son would be here shortly; he had taken his father's death very hard and she had promised him they would do everything they could to bring closure to this case. She only hoped they could.

* * * * *

Jon left the sheriff's office after filing his missing person's report, he paused as he stepped out into the glare. He didn't feel better; he thought he would. He felt worse. Dread was what he was really experiencing. Where was Cole? He had a feeling that this wasn't going to turn out well; this wasn't the story he wanted to write. Cole was his friend. What he needed now was to talk to his dad.

As he sat in the car with the A/C on high he punched in his father's number. "Hey Dad, Jon here," he said.

"Jon, good to hear from you," his father answered.

"Just thought I'd check in, let you know I'm alright."

"Good," his father hesitated. "Do I sense a 'but' coming on?"

"You always could read me, that's why I could never get away with anything when I was a teenager," Jon laughed.

"Yes, that's what fathers do. When are you coming up to see me? Or do I have to come down there?"

Samuel Albee was a busy man, president and CEO of Albee Chemicals, owner of several car agencies, and active in local politics. His life in Chicago was successful. But what he wanted most was his son there, in business with him.

Jon was as independent as his father. But his father's dream of his only son following him in business was shattered when Jon announced early in college, he wanted to be a journalist. Samuel encouraged him anyway, all the while hoping it was a passing fancy. After about 10 years or so he had come to accept his son, the journalist.

Jon loved his father for never pressuring him to join his business. They visited each other often, but Samuel knew his son and right now he sensed Jon wanted his help on something very important to him.

* * * * *

Otto, George and Tom were here. The receptionist directed each one to a separate conference room. Willa entered room number three to talk to Otto. Otto rose, ever the gentleman. "Good to see you Willa," he said holding out his hand.

She shook it and said, "Please have a seat. I'm terribly sorry about your friend, Luther. We will do everything possible to find out what happened. Let's start, again, with yesterday morning."

"Okay ... We meet at McDonald's five or six mornings a week. If any of us are not going to make it, we let someone know. It's sort of like a wellness check. George is married but Tom, Luther, and I aren't." Otto paused; looked at Willa. "You see me sometimes on the beach; I'm there almost every morning early before I go for coffee."

Willa nodded as she made notes, she had already heard this story, but it never hurts to hear it again. "And yesterday morning?" she prodded.

"Luther never showed, so about nine, George said, something is wrong let's go check on him. So, we did. We had called him several times and each time his phone went directly to voice mail." Otto hesitated, shaking his head reliving those moments. "We all jumped in George's SUV, it only took a few minutes to get there. Oh boy," his voice was strained, his eyes were red, "this is so bad."

He looked up and right into Willa eyes. She stared back at him. This man that still looked at the world as an exciting place, a place where he found treasures walking the beach; not dead friends. A place where he had friends that shared many things, a place where evil had suddenly cropped up, a place he had never known before.

His hands came up to shield his face, as if to protect it from what he was revealing. Willa offered him a tissue. "His truck door was open; we parked right behind it. We were laughing, joking, saying, he must be losing it. And then we opened his front door."

Willa knew this was hard for him. It was hard for her and she already knew evil existed all around. She knew she must find the source of such a horrible act. "Take your time, Otto, you are doing fine," she calmly interjected.

"The stench almost knocked us over. George, well, he knew what it was. He shut the door and called 9-1-1," Otto closed his eyes, as if to blot out the scene. "George is a good man, smart, a little too smart sometimes, but his experience kicked in and he took control. He shut the door, called for help, and kept us away from the scene."

Willa didn't know George when he was a detective, only as a retiree and the father of Kevin. She had heard some pretty wild stories about this past employee; she only believed half of them. She had listened to Kevin talk about his dad with mixed emotions. First, she could tell Kevin loved his dad and he became a detective because of him. Second, he was struggling, trying to be his own man. Which was hard when you had to follow in the footsteps of a man like George Vasser.

Otto continued to tell Willa about the previous day and Luther's plans to go fishing. When they were finished and walked outside the room everyone was waiting for them.

"If you remember anything else, please call." Russell instructed them. "We are working hard to find a motive; we hope to find justice for your friend." All three walked out as Russell, Kevin, and Willa headed for the back of the room to compare notes.

Barbara Marvin

Chapter 11

Willa worked best under pressure, and right now she felt a sense of pressure. They needed another look at the crime scene and Kevin was the designated driver. The ride was unusually quiet as he stopped the car just off Stickney Point road, at the end of the driveway.

Willa, Kevin, and Russell, each lost in their own thoughts, gazed at the very neat mobile home. Except for the very obvious yellow tape restricting anyone from intruding, the tire tracks from the barrage of emergency vehicles that had responded and parked on the other-wise well-kept lawn, it was your typical mobile home.

Willa conjured up images of Luther mowing, weeding, and raking. He was meticulous. Yesterday she had noted his storage shed would pass the white glove test. He would be horrified if he could see it now. She was becoming personally involved, this was too personal. Death has a strange way of showing the world an inner being; things not considered before were now important.

Deep logic and years of experience automatically kicked in as Willa began to analyze the situation. Maybe this was why she was so good at her job. Her intuition seemed to take effect just when she needed it. She paused momentarily before ducking under the yellow tape. Kevin and Russell were both studying the entrance and knew Willa well enough to let her be, at least for a few more minutes.

The small living room was covered with dark smudges where technicians had lifted prints. It was just like they left it yesterday. Except for the smudges and one other very important fact; today all was quiet. Willa could feel Luther, she could feel the terror, the pain; she just couldn't feel the perpetrator or the reason behind this slaughter. Oh, she was sure it was something Luther did or more likely, something the killer thought Luther saw or did, but she was not getting any sense of what that could be.

"Okay," Willa said slowly. "Luther came home from fishing. I believe he was accosted in the carport. His truck door was left open. Definitely not like him"

"And he left his fish in the back of the truck," Kevin added. "My dad said he never brought his undressed fish home; too messy for him. So, we must assume something happened at the marina, something that was so shocking he forgot to clean his catch. He left the dock in a hurry."

"If he was stopped as he got out of his truck, someone followed him home or was waiting for him here. Either way, he didn't see them until it was too late. He is parked perfectly in the carport, like he did every day. Therefore, he didn't know anyone was here until he got out of his truck."

Looking at the report in her hand, Willa said, "Nothing appeared to be stolen. His wallet is here, with credit cards and cash. He had three hundred dollars in a kitchen drawer. Definitely not a robbery."

"Yeah, and his fishing bag still contained his binoculars and his cell phone. Too bad the binoculars weren't a camera." Russell added.

"That gives me an idea. Did we check his phone?" Kevin's eyes lit up.

"Yes! He hadn't had any calls before your dad's calls that morning." Willa responded.

"I meant did we check his phone for pictures?" Kevin was already dialing Frank back at the office.

* * * * *

Jon found it difficult to concentrate all day. His mind was so absorbed with his friend. By quitting time, he was running on auto-pilot. He and Cole had become good friends in the few short years they had known each other; they shared a lot. Stories of girlfriends, of which neither had right now. Stories of teen years, both had tried drugs. Jon liked to be in control and felt drugs left him vulnerable, so it became a thing of the past. Cole still indulged occasionally.

Cole had taken on-line courses trying to find something that he liked, something that he could call a major, but had floundered when it came time to actually find a job in one of those fields. Whereas, Jon went to a prestigious college and changed his major to journalism from business, knowing exactly what he wanted to do.

Jon pulled into the parking lot at Big Bart's, hesitating just a moment; he opened the car door and stepped out. He hoped this stop would make him feel better. Still early, still light out, he glanced around the parking lot, well aware it was nearly empty.

The locals had not yet arrived; this would be easier for him since he wanted to talk to Big Bart, alone. His hand pushed the dirty front door; it opened easily. Standing inside he waited for his eyes to become accustom to the dark interior, then he strode to the far end of the bar, pulled out a stool, and sat.

Big Bart himself was tending bar tonight. "What'll it be, Jon?" he said.

Jon looked around. "Where's your new bartender?"

"Oh, he didn't work out. This town is too small for him, he decided to try a big city. I think he headed to Miami!"

"Hmm, I'll have a beer."

Bart put the beer and a glass in front of Jon. Jon pushed the glass away. "Save the glass, I don't need it." He never drank from a glass in places like this. He wasn't sure how clean they were. He was really paranoid about dirty glasses. "Big Bart," Jon was determined to ask him things that were on his mind. Inside he felt a tingle, this sometimes happened when he had a big story. Was this a big story? "Have you seen Cole? Have you heard from him?"

Bart stopped wiping the bar, looked right at Jon and replied. "No, I haven't. I'm a little worried about him. Where do you think he went?" Bart's expression had gone from a smile to a frown and any expectations of information left with it.

"I don't know, but wherever he is, he left his truck behind... and his cell phone."

"No kidding!" Bart exclaimed as he moved down the bar away from Jon; wiping as he went. "That is strange... Let me know if you hear from him," he added.

The hair on the back of Jon's neck stood up. He nodded as he opened his wallet and extracted four one-dollar bills and laid them on the bar. Without another word, he walked out. The tingle was even greater than earlier, and he didn't feel better at all.

* * * * *

It was late when Willa wrapped it up for the day. Her mind couldn't let go of all she had learned or was it all she didn't learn. They were no farther along on this case now than they had been earlier.

Driving home, she slowed as she passed Luther's residence, slowing again, as she passed the marina, noting the marina was a short ride from Luther's home. Continuing, she took another fifteen minutes to reach her home. As she pulled into her driveway the security light came on, cutting a swath through the darkness. In her garage, she quickly closed the door and her eyes, briefly. She had not realized how tired she was until now. Her mind was wrapped around the job she now owned, causing her to forget to stop for a sandwich or anything else.

"Guess I'll have to cook something, ugh," she murmured to herself as she opened the car door. The kitchen was the first room she came to after punching in the security code on the alarm system and unlocking the door to enter the house. Looking around for something to eat wasn't helping. Automatically she headed for the sofa in the living room. She flopped down knowing this was a mistake. If she sat here another minute she would just be here all night. It would be so easy for her to close her eyes and sleep.

Then she realized she knew where to get a bite to eat at this time of night without cooking something herself. She retraced her steps; kitchen, mud room, garage, car. She backed out of the driveway with a plan in mind and a little renewed energy. Lonnie's was north of Sarasota, a place she and Russell found by accident one night looking for a quiet place to have a drink, talk, and not be interrupted by any personnel from the office. Sarasota wasn't a small town, but sometimes it was impossible to have an intimate moment in a public place, Lonnie's turned out to be a great find.

She had been coming here ever since. Lonnie was now a friend; her bar was a hangout for family types. Lonnie didn't have much use for anyone causing a scene. She was a no-nonsense tough girl, and everyone respected that. She liked Willa and Russell right from the start and "it never hurt to have the law on your side," she said.

Tonight, Willa wanted to just sit and converse with someone about anything, except the case. The buzz was soft as she entered; a couple of guys she recognized were playing pool. They waved, she waved back. She walked to the rear of the bar, mostly out of habit and sat with her back to the wall facing the front door. Guess it was a cop thing.

Lonnie looked up and smiled. "Hey Willa, you look like you could use a drink. Where are your followers?"

"Hi girlfriend. I'm all alone tonight." She answered.

Lonnie pulled a tall glass from the overhead rack, filled it with ice, added a shot of vodka and finished off with tonic and a slice of lime. "Here's a little something to put some color back in those lovely cheeks."

"Thanks. Kinda slow tonight?" she noticed, glancing around. Lonnie's was a place Willa felt contented. She felt comfortable with Lonnie and Lonnie made sure she had the respect and privacy she wanted and needed.

"What's going on with you? Are you working the case of the old guy found dead near Stickney Point Road?" Lonnie said coming out from behind the bar and sitting beside her.

"Oh yeah, … really a strange one. We are trying to develop some leads," Willa's brow knotted. "Have you heard anything? Anything at all."

"No, nothing. It isn't gathering much interest with anyone here. Just another senior citizen whose time has come."

"Well that's not how we see it. Although nothing in his life so far has turned up a motive. Nothing worth dying for. No enemies... that we have found. Let's change the subject. What's new with you, any new men in your life? Or any new life in your men?"

"Heck no! I'm in a draught! What do you suggest?" Lonnie was never in a draught, she was just very selective.

"You're asking me? Ha, I can't keep my own life in order." They both laughed and then were quiet.

Lonnie picked up the phone and called the shop next door to order two sandwiches. The owner was closed but agreed to deliver them anyway. This wasn't new to Lonnie, she had done this on several occasions with Willa and knew this was why Willa was here.

After eating, Willa dragged herself off the stool. "Hate to eat and run but I'm beat, see you later," she apologized before heading out the door for home. The ride back was filled with brooding thoughts of Luther; she hardly noticed the traffic. She did notice the car parked in her driveway. She recognized it; hit the garage door opener, pulled in, and waited for just a minute.

Willa noticed the gulf was much calmer tonight and the moon was a white glow behind a few clouds. Maybe this was an omen, she thought.

"Hey Willa," Russ greeted her.

"How long you been sitting there?"

"Not long. I was going to give you another five minutes and then leave a note," he wasn't smiling as he walked up to her car.

She opened the door and took his hand as she got out. "You could have called, you know?"

"Yeah, I know. Can I come in?" he smiled now looking at the closing garage door. Willa smiled too.

She keyed in the security code on the alarm, unlocked the door, and walked into the kitchen for the second time tonight. "Okay; what's going on? Can I get you something to drink?" Opening the refrigerator, she looked at Russ as he made himself at home sitting at the kitchen table.

"I have iced tea, coke, something stronger... I can make a pot of coffee!"

"I'll have iced tea," he replied his eyes never leaving her.

She knew he wondered where she had been but thought she would let him wonder a little longer.

"It's good to see you tonight, Russ. Are you here to talk about Luther?"

"Yes, and no!" he said.

"Okay," she paused, handing him his drink.

"Willa, I know we can't go back and undo what's been done. I know I reacted badly to an even worse situation... I'm ready to apologize. If you can accept it?"

Willa still carried the guilt of her own behavior last year when her ex-husband was found murdered. He had been living right under her nose, leading a double life and the reality of this threw her for a loop. She left town without telling anyone. She went back to Atlanta, her home town, and was eventually instrumental in helping to solve the case. Almost losing her job, her friends, her self-respect, and Russell; the man she loved, in the process.

All actions she was sorry for. Regaining her job had been easier than it should have been. But, her personal life was still in shambles. What would tonight bring?

Chapter 12

Jon sat in his car, hands on the wheel, but unable to take his eyes off Big Bart's Hillbilly Bar. The thoughts plaguing him were all about the lack of concern he felt coming from Big Bart, and why? Bart had professed that he felt like a father to Cole, gave him space to write his book, had his picture on the wall, and practically gave him the boat he used. At one time he had loaned him money and pulled a few strings to get his driver's license back after a DUI.

Now, he seemed unconcerned that Cole was missing, offered nothing in the way of help, no clue where he might have gone, or a fear that something may have happened to him. Did he know something no one else did? Jon shook his head; he just didn't understand it.

He made a mental note to call Lisa at the sheriff's office tomorrow morning because right now his mission was to help his friend. To do that would require his ability to involve law enforcement. They were not concerned that an adult wasn't where someone thought he should be. Simple as that. He would change that!

Finally, he started the car and slowly left the lot, feeling that Big Bart knew much more than he was sharing. Traffic was heavy, but he hardly noticed. Pulling into the apartment complex, a vision of Cole in his mind caused a dreadful feeling to envelope him.

Everything looked the same; he parked in the space right beside Cole's truck. He could see a note stuffed in the crack of the door. Quickly, stepping over leaves, pine cones, and other debris blowing around him in the parking lot, he rushed to the door. The note was from the sheriff's department asking Cole to give them a call. At least they had been here. A lot of good that did! He stuck the note back where he had found it. Next stop, the slip where his boat was.

South of Cole's apartment, in an older part of town, Cole had rented a slip; a small space to keep his boat. Jon knew it well. The boat was tied up... just the way Cole always left it. No sign of any activity near here. The dock wasn't the best. A missing plank or two made you cautious, so Jon extracted his flashlight, carefully stepping into the 14-footer, he pointed the beam of light under the small seat, on the floor, and into every crevice. Nothing out of place - no blood, no soiled clothing, no bait bucket. Nothing. Cole loved his boat. It was way neater than his apartment would ever be.

"Damn you Cole! Where are you?" he swore out loud. "You didn't just decide to vanish, did you?" Jon raised his head and saw a figure approaching him, he carefully pointed his light in that direction.

"Hey! What are you doing?" came the question from that silhouette.

"Hi, I'm Jon... Cole's friend," he answered.

The man continued to approach. He appeared to be in his fifties, old jeans with a faded t-shirt, and a lean face with a scraggly beard.

"Oh, okay, where's Cole?" the man asked.

"You must be Henry Brewer," Jon said.

"Yeah... I remember you. You came here a few times with Cole."

"Yes. Let me ask you a question, Henry. Have you seen Cole lately?"

"No, but I saw you here and Cole usually stops by my house if he is out here after dark. So, I wondered what was going on."

"No one has seen him for a few days," Jon paused as he pulled his business card from his shirt pocket. "Would you call me if you hear from him?"

"Sure, if I see him before you do." Henry turned around and walked through the dark back the way he had come.

Jon had sensed all along that something had happened to Cole and now he was sure. But where and how and the biggest question in his mind - WHY?

He needed to pull himself out of this funk. Action, belief, clarification, ABC - This was how he worked. Shifting gears to a different state of mind, he started formulating his plan to find some answers. He left the boat just as he found it, made his way to his car and headed home.

The high-rise across from Ringling Causeway had been his home since he moved here, a gift from his father. At times, he felt out of place, because the average age of the other owners was at least sixty-five or seventy. Right now, he needed a place to concentrate, to put together an outline. And this would be the perfect place. He needed to be taken seriously by law enforcement. If a grown man wants to drop out of sight, that's his right. This was something more. Much more. He wouldn't stop until he had answers.

* * * * *

It seemed like a lifetime to Willa since she and Russell had used her home as an extended office. Russell seemed to fall back to those earlier times and was as much at home as he ever was. However, Willa needed to settle something before she could work this close to him. Looking at him in his tight faded jeans made her mind jump to other times. Tonight, she was guided by different instincts.

Willa wasn't sure she was ready to come to grips with that part of her life. It had been almost a year since a large part of her personal life had been unmasked. She was a guarded person trying to live on the outside like she was expected, trying to be someone she wasn't. Living with an abusive father had left many scars. They may be invisible to everyone, but not to her; she could plainly see the little warts she was trying to hide.

She was hoping this night, she might have a chance to rekindle what had left a hole in her heart. She wanted so much from Russell, but her self-depreciation would not allow her to admit it could be a possibility. Years of therapy hadn't done the job, what made her think things could change now?

"You don't know..." she began. "You don't know how much I've missed what we had. What I thought we had." In speaking those words, she was putting herself at risk. Not like her at all.

"Willa, let me say this. I don't really know you. I, ah, only know what you share. But I know what I think of you. I know what I need from you. I know what I want from you."

"Russ." Willa's voice was barely audible. "Let me say, I'm sorry for everything I put you through. I'm sorry I didn't confide in you. I'm sorry for many, many things. I never wanted to see the pain in your eyes or watch you struggle with your feelings. Can we maybe, just maybe... get back some of what we had. The best thing that I ever had in my life was you."

Russell's long wait in her driveway earlier was the only place he could go tonight. It didn't matter how long he waited. He knew they needed to work close on this case and it would be impossible if she didn't realize how he felt. Yes, he had been hurt by her when she left town, when she left him out of her life. But, they say 'time heals all wounds'. He knew she came with a lot of scars. He accepted them, now. Or at least he hoped he did. As much as he would rather not, Russ knew they needed to talk about these issues.

The silence was loud. Then he smiled, the smile she could never resist. Maybe life was giving her a second chance. She knew she didn't deserve it, but she was going to try.

They had so much work to do; the pages of her diary would be filled tonight. OK, so she really didn't have a diary, she thought, but if she did …

* * * * *

The next morning in the office, Willa, Russell, and Kevin had been working for hours when Lisa left her desk and walked back to stand near them. Hands on her hips she said, "Question! Who wants to talk to Jon Albee?" Silence. "Don't everyone volunteer at once."

"What's he want? To interview one of us? Let me tell you, we don't need that journalist beating up on us right now. We have enough to do without that. Besides, we are all busy," Russell stated and then buried his head in his work.

"Hey! It's not that. His friend Cole is still missing. He wants to talk to someone to see if anything has been discovered since he first reported it," Lisa explained.

"Okay, Willa you take it," Kevin stated with a grin that looked painted on.

"Why me?" she retorted.

"Because ... you're the right gender."

"Hey, guys, sorry Willa. Jon looks serious," Lisa said as she chastised them. "Give him a break. I don't really know what's going on, but he can tell you, okay?"

"Put him in two. I'll be right there." Willa gave in and turned to Kevin, "Right gender? I guess I'll have to kick your ass to show you it's no longer a man's world." Grinning just as big as she could, she walked towards the conference room.

"Hi, Jon. Have a seat," she offered, getting serious.

"Willa, thanks for seeing me," Jon said. "I know you are busy, but can you tell me what you've learned about Cole?"

Willa sat at the table and motioned Jon to sit. She could see he was in a very agitated state. She had never seen him quite like this. But, she needed to hurry this along.

"Jon, we haven't been able to locate him. We sent someone out to his place, he wasn't there. I'm waiting to hear from him."

"I know," he interrupted. "I don't think you are going to hear from him. Something has happened to him. This isn't like him."

"Okay," she paused. "Let's hear what you are thinking."

Jon was very organized, and he understood the basic workings of the sheriff's office. He understood how hard it was for one adult to classify another as missing. He was prepared to present his case; to demand, if necessary, that Cole be labeled missing. That would start an official search for him. "This is what I've got." He opened his notebook.

Willa was impressed as she glanced across the table.

"Well. First of all, Cole missed his book signing. This was a big deal for him. No explanation, just no show. Second, he doesn't go anywhere without his phone, it's in his apartment. Third, his boat is moored at the dock. Fourth, his truck is parked in front of his place. And fifth, no one and I mean no one, has seen or heard from him." Jon paused, looking Willa right in the eyes he said, "And, the other day when I was interviewing him for a story he said he had had a death threat."

Jon took a breath. "I have to say I didn't believe him, and he dropped it. I thought he was... well, fabricating a little excitement for the blurb I was writing for the paper. After all, it is a murder book."

This got Willa's full attention.

"What else did he say?"

"Nothing about that. He was drinking pretty heavily, so was I. We parted ways in Big Bart's parking lot. And I haven't seen him since."

"Okay Jon. I've taken some notes, I'll keep in touch. Now we have a place to start. And, let me add. I know you were good friends and I'm sorry about this. We'll get on it."

Jon nodded his head.

Willa got Cole's boat slip address and his cell number. Reaching for his hand and shaking it, she said, "Thanks for coming in Jon. We'll call you soon. But, feel free to call if you think of anything else. As of today, Cole is officially missing"

Jon was feeling better about this meeting, but not about his friend. Now it seemed as if law enforcement was taking him seriously and would help solve the mystery. "Thank you, I will and don't worry, I will be in touch."

Chapter 13

It had been days since the murder of Luther Landrow; today's paper was still carrying the story on the front-page, bottom half. Jon had insisted, and since this was a very slow news day he got his way.

After talking at length with Landrow's son, the only new details covered were personal. Landrow was typical of area senior citizens. Jon elaborated on his retirement, hobbies, and past life. His past life was as uneventful as his retirement. His health was good up until his death and he had friends, including a retired detective. He had gotten nothing new from the detectives.

Jon didn't know how long he could convince his boss to carry this on the front page; he supposed, until the next big thing. It made him stop and ponder, are we only important until something else occurs? Being a journalist, he realized he knew the answer to that.

He was still using his own time to keep the search for Cole going. Cole was a different story; but in reality, Luther and Cole were similar. Both were gone, and no one knew what happened to either. Until Cole was found, Jon felt a hole in his heart that he knew would just get bigger each day until he had an answer. He would not let it go, he owed Cole that much.

* * * * *

Captain Dunbar was waiting for everyone to take a seat. His office continued to be the setting for these early meetings each day. "Have a seat," he directed almost distracted from the business at hand.

Willa, Russell, Kevin and Frank once again, found seats at the small table in the back of his private office. "Frank, how are you coming with the pictures on the phone?" Dunbar asked, still standing. Looking at his staff, he pulled out the last chair and sat.

Willa felt something else was at the root of Cap's look of frustration. She hoped it wasn't her. For some reason he kept glaring at her.

"I'm working on them. There are two, both are very dark. Technology might allow me to lighten the images enough to get some information. I'll let you know just as soon as I can." Frank reported.

"The background check turned up nothing." Russell added. "This man had absolutely nothing in his life that would even suggest this could happen. And his family are all pretty upstanding people and fairly boring."

"Well this was not a random act of violence. Someone did this for a reason; unless it was mistaken identity. Could that be the case?" Kevin said half-heartedly.

Willa had an idea and it was the only feasible cause at this point. "Something happened while he was fishing!" she suggested.

"Maybe he saw drugs being smuggled in. Maybe we should see if we can locate the area where he was fishing and the area he took the pictures," Kevin was taking notes and speaking at the same time.

"I'm all for that!" Willa said as Russell nodded.

"I'm sure my Dad knows a few of Landrow's fishing spots. I'll call him. Then we can head out. Who has a boat?" Kevin closed his notebook and laid his pen on the top.

"I can get one," Russell offered. "A buddy of mine has this great little fishing boat; we just used it over at Okeechobee. He'll let us use it. Then we won't have to get any other agency involved."

"Cap, are you alright?" Willa asked.

"Yeah, I'm fine, just get this thing solved, will ya," he dismissed them and moved to his desk.

Willa hung back, as everyone else left the office.

"Go on, get out of here!" Cap snapped, looking straight at her.

Willa stared back, turned and walked to the door, closed it, and walked back to stand in front of the captain. "Cap... I know something is wrong. What is it?"

He motioned her to leave.

"No, not until you tell me what's going on!" she blurted out, surprised at herself for confronting her boss like that.

"Hell, Willa, sit down."

Pulling the chair directly in front of him she waited. "If I've done something," she started.

Cap held up his hand to stop her. Speaking slowly, he started, "Politics are not easy." He folded his hands in front of him; she waited, he would get it out. She knew him well enough. He was a good man, had come up through the ranks. Sometimes too good.

He wasn't smiling. "Willa. I'm going to share this with you. And if you share it with anyone, anyone, you are through here. Understand?"

She didn't know what to expect now. She was hoping it was about his review board meeting coming up or about the cut in funding for the department's budget. What had she gotten herself into? "Okay. I'm here. What's going on?" she said waiting for the panic to ease up.

Captain glanced at the closed door; then he shifted his eyes to the tinted windows that lit up this office. "My ass is on the line," he paused for just a moment. Then, as if he had opened the flood gates, he started talking.

Willa knew they had many issues here; some were of her making. Quickly she recalled the mess she stirred up when her ex-husband died. She had disobeyed orders to stay away from the case. She didn't listen; she went to Atlanta without permission and almost got herself killed. She put her whole team at risk. In the end she solved the case, but almost lost her job and the respect of her co-workers in the process. Eventually Cap came around. I'm still working, and things are getting back to normal, she thought. She never thought Dunbar would have to put his job on the line for her, but he did. He was on probation; and now a high roller was calling in markers. He wanted Cap to step down or fire her. This high roller, whose name no one knew, was seeking revenge.

"Why now?" she asked.

"I'm not sure," he replied. "I only know my review is scheduled next month. One of us will be gone."

Willa was an emotional wreck, she wasn't showing it, but she was. "I can leave, Cap…"

"Don't even think about that; you are a great detective and I, we need you. I will work through this," he laced his fingers in front of his chest, pressed hard. She heard them pop. "But… you can do me a favor…"

"Sure, anything," she quickly said.

"Solve this case, pull out all the stops, show the," he pointed up, indicating the upper level offices several stories higher, "and I don't mean the man upstairs, I mean the man up the stairs in this building. Show him we can do this. Make this an example of teamwork, hard work, smart work! Just get it done!"

"Okay"

"Now. Get out of here!" He stood to indicate this conversation was over.

Willa left without smiling, as Captain Dunbar stared out the tinted window into the space before him.

Chapter 14

There was no smile on Jon's face as he scanned the men sitting at the bar. The man he saw was older; he could tell by the touch of gray in his hair. His attire suggested he wasn't from around here. This was the Marina Bar and the patrons were in boating gear; all except him.

His sport coat was expensive, Jon knew expensive when he saw it. Looking in the mirror behind the bar Jon couldn't see his face as his head was down, checking his phone; but it was who he was looking for.

"Mr. Brookfield?" Jon asked standing behind him.

The man looked up, turned, and smiled. "You must be Jon Albee. Call me Earl."

The men sized each other up as they shook hands. "Let's move to a table!" Jon said moving away from the bar.

Earl pulled out his wallet and threw twenty dollars on the bar, and then followed Jon to a table overlooking the bay. "Your father is a friend of mine. He says you need my help," Earl got right to the point.

Jon nodded his head. "Yes I do, I think."

"Okay, tell me what I can do for you."

Jon opened up his briefcase.

* * * * *

Willa went straight to her desk; she didn't look at any of her co-workers. She stared at the open three-ring binder in front of her. The murder book, as it was known, was not at all complete. It had few pages; not nearly enough. A murder book is the black and white of the investigation. It contains all crime scene photos and sketches, autopsy and forensic reports, witness statements, investigators' notes, everything. It begins with the first report of a murder and isn't closed until a suspect is arrested.

What do you do when nothing seems to offer any clues, she thought. All the while she could feel the glares of Kevin and Russell. Lucky for her Frank was too preoccupied to look her way.

"Okay everyone," Russell announced loud and clear, "Who's going with me fishing... for clues?"

"Count me in," Kevin said.

"I'm too busy here, you can go without me. Besides I can't swim." Frank answered.

"You can't swim? You can't swim? I never knew anyone in this town who couldn't swim." Kevin chided him.

Willa watched the bantering back and forth. "I can swim, I'm going!"

"Good. You have to wear your bikini." Kevin added leering at her.

She gave him a dirty look and turned toward the receptionist who was calling her name.

"Willa, got a minute? Someone is here to see you." June announced.

"Russ, can you and Kevin wait a minute? Let me see what this is about. Then I'll be with you." Willa asked, walking toward the reception area

"Yeah, no problem," Russell replied.

Willa didn't recognize the man standing there as she put out her hand and said, "Hello, I'm Detective Dupree."

He shook her hand and answered, "My name is Earl Brookfield. I'd like to talk to you."

"Well, certainly. Just step in the conference room. Please have a seat. I'll be right back."

She returned to her desk to pick up her note pad and to give Russ and Kevin a quick heads up.

"This shouldn't take long," she told them.

Sitting down across from Earl she knew he wasn't local. But he was a professional, attorney maybe, what else? "Okay Mr.

Brookfield, what do you want to talk to me about?"

"Here is my card," he replied, handing her a slick embossed business card. She glanced at it. It contained his name and two phone numbers. She racked her brain trying to place the 312-area code.

"I'm from Chicago," he said as Willa nodded. Yes, Chicago she thought. Okay. "I'm a private investigator; I've been hired by Jon Albee, actually Jon's father, Samuel." As he talked, Willa was puzzled. "I know I have no jurisdiction in your state, so I'm looking for someone local. A licensed PI. Someone that gets along well with the sheriff's office, if you know what I mean. Someone I can work with. Someone I can hire. Who would you suggest?"

"Come again. You are working for Jon Albee on what?"

"Oh, I'm sorry. Jon's friend Cole Mitchell seems to be missing. I've been hired to locate him and in order to do this, legally, I'll need work with a local agency, which is licensed in Florida." Earl retrieved a note pad and pen from the inside of his expensive sport coat.

151

"Okay," Willa said. "I'm just surprised to see where Jon has gone on this. He filed a missing person's report; but you know yourself, adults can leave anytime they want. We have no sign of foul play, no behavior that might even suggest it. As for local PI's I'll give you a list. We don't recommend anyone. Some are less obnoxious than others." She smiled. "You can interview them and make your own choice."

Earl smiled back; he liked her already. She was to the point and she wasn't bad to look at. "I'll do that," he stated. After flipping a few pages in his note pad he looked at Willa. "Cole left his truck, his cell phone, his boat and missed a very important book signing. Wouldn't that give you cause to believe he was missing?"

"No, it doesn't. But, like I say, you are free to check it out." Willa turned the card over in her hand and jotted a name on the back. Then stood up, "Let us know if you find anything that involves any illegal activity. If that's all you need, I'll get you those names now," she said as she started for the door.

"I'm quite busy today, nice to meet you and good luck."

After Earl had left, both Russ and Kevin looked expectantly at her.

"What?" She asked.

"Well, what was that all about?" Kevin asked

"He's a PI from Chicago; he was hired by Jon Albee," she shared, still stunned that Jon would go this far. "I think this Cole thing just got serious."

Chapter 15

The sun was setting out over the gulf when Jon pulled into the parking lot at Sandy Beach Club on Midnight Pass Road. It had been the spot he preferred until his friendship with Cole took him to Big Bart's. He would still choose this place over Bart's any day except he enjoyed his relationship with Cole enough to put it on hold.

There was no comparison between the two. Sandy Beach had no dart board, no pool table, and no clientele that looked like they just stepped out of a remake of *Deliverance*. What it did have was a clean, well-lit bar, and lots of windows featuring a gulf view. Most customers were in shorts or bathing suits. They had an outside Tiki bar where you didn't even have to leave the beach. The menu was limited, but the food good; boasting a French Chef.

Jon saw Earl arrive in his rental car, so he waited for him by the door. "I have to sit by the window; I love this view. It's refreshing, and boy do I need it, now." Earl quickly informed Jon.

Jon looked at him and smiled. "Welcome to the Sunshine State."

"Jon, let me tell you, I've never backed down from a fight, never quit until the truth was out. But today, after connecting with a guy named Silas, from the agency I'll be working with, by the way; I'm learning of a whole new world." The grin on his face looked forced; out of place.

"What does that mean?" Jon asked, not knowing if he should laugh or be worried.

"Well, there are a few places I can't go. One of them I believe played a part in Cole's disappearance. First, let me say, I believe Cole did not leave of his own accord; that said, I don't know if he was forced to leave or if he is dead."

"Thanks Earl." Jon was quiet for a minute, his mind trying to grasp this, something he had refused to consider until now. "I know the sheriff's office is hesitant to put any effort into this. That's why I have you."

Earl had had a busy day, mostly learning about this town and its citizens. After reporting the few facts about Cole, they were ready for some heavy lifting. Of course, they couldn't do it on an empty stomach. They decided to have dinner first and then formulate a plan.

* * * * *

Willa, Russ, and Kevin pulled into the driveway of Russ's friend. There was the boat, as promised, with the trailer already attached to the pick-up truck. All they had to do was drive. Russ drove the truck and Kevin and Willa followed in the car.

Russ launched the boat with ease. He had done this many times and he easily maneuvered the 14-footer to the ramp side of the dock as Willa changed shoes. Her Nike's gave her a little comfort as she was not looking forward to this excursion. She was never a fisherman or a boat lover. But she refused to show it. No need to give the guys any ammo to pick on her with.

"Okay, which way first?" Russ asked cranking up the 30-horse power engine. This boat could hold the three of them as long as they weren't moving around. Willa wouldn't be moving much. She was wishing she had stayed on the dock or better yet, back at the office with Frank.

"Let's start north and work our way back. My dad said Luther fished up and down this side of the bay." Kevin quickly added.

All eyes scanned the other side. Many homes were built in this beautiful area. Most were old mansion style buildings with newer docks and piers. Some very elaborate; others more modest but still out of the price range of your top-notch detectives.

Russell drove slow allowing them to check out everyone. The motor was loud, so their speaking was kept to a minimum. They spent the better part of an hour studying both sides of the bay, north of the marina and still nothing that looked like the images on the pictures.

It had been high tide when Luther took the pictures, today the tide would not crest until later. They took that into consideration and were looking at docks with lower water levels. It was getting frustrating, nothing close to what they expected to see.

"Hey, Russ, let's go south, past the marina for a while." Kevin said over the roar of the motor.

Russ gave a thumbs up as he turned the boat around.

Willa had not gotten into the swing of things. However, her concentration was at an all-time high. She never understood the need for men to fish so much. She was glad she wasn't having motion sickness. This was the last time she would be on a boat, if she had anything to say about it.

After they passed the marina, Russ slowed down. With renewed interest Kevin sat up and pointed across the bay. Willa remained in her seat. She saw what they were looking at. They were seeing the dock of interest; and then the next one looked just like it, and the next one. They were all alike; most likely built by the same builder. But they felt they were in the general area of the pictures. A closer look was needed.

At this point Russell headed across the bay to get closer to the docks; not wanting to attract attention, they didn't stop. Cruising by all three docks one by one. These spacious homes had expansive lawns and many trees between the piers and the buildings themselves making it difficult to see a number or name to identify the docks' locations or owners.

All three buildings were stately, part of the older more affluent section of the key they were on. Not able to see any fencing between the homes, Willa wondered if this was what they were looking for. Then she spied a number on one of the garages. All three appeared to be empty or at least no outside activity. They took pictures quickly with their phones.

Russell continued a little farther to hide the fact that they were looking at those docks. Then he turned the boat toward the marina and continued back. Next thing on the agenda, determine why Luther felt compelled to photograph these docks at night. Maybe they had found the location of the pictures. Now they had a starting point.

Chapter 16

At the office the mood had improved somewhat. It was the first bit of evidence; a possible location of the site where the photographs were taken. Did the pictures have anything to do with Luther's death? Could be the image of the dock wasn't what he was aiming at. Maybe he was trying to catch a picture of ... say, a shark in the water; or maybe it was his finger on the wrong button on the phone. There were several reasons the pictures may not be as important as they felt.

Until the possibility was eliminated, Willa would work on a connection to the photos and the crime. It was all they had. "Frank, how are you coming on that property ownership?" Willa asked.

"Funny thing happened on the way to the ... sorry. Look at this. This one is owned by DIL or Diverse Investments Limited. When I researched that I got a list of officers of the company. Nothing stands out." Frank wasn't easily puzzled, but the look in his face told a different story now.

At this point he went back to searching for the owners of the two adjacent properties. And was he surprised! All three were owned by the same Delaware Corporation. "I'll contact them," he added, already deep into his search.

* * * * *

Earl couldn't even smile. He had been a PI for twenty years; but that was in Chicago. The only time he had been in Florida was for vacation; several times to Orlando with his family, when they were younger. And once he went to West Palm Beach with a group of guys looking for fun before he got married. That time had been the poster child for Florida vacations. Nothing but beaches, fishing, and relaxing. Oh yeah, and golf.

Sarasota had the reputation for the whitest beaches with great restaurants, museums, and other attractions. Not to mention friendly people. Now he was seeing the other side. The underbelly, the part the Chamber of Commerce refused to acknowledge. The part that made his mind and body come to full attention.

He had seen worse at home. This sort of thing was expected in the big cities, in Chicago. Here he didn't know it existed, that is until now. He was unprepared for it and it made him mad that he had been caught off guard. It seems this town had many secrets and he was ready to uncover them all.

As his mind switched gears, he thought of that hot detective he had seen today; she was in a boat cruising by the dock where he was checking out Cole's boat. She was accompanied by two other detectives and he knew it wasn't a pleasure trip. Had they started looking for Cole? Even though he was sure that wasn't the case; he was sure it was all business.

He had watched as they slowly made their way north, then south. He continued checking every inch of the boat, his reason for being there. Nothing to indicate Cole had used it recently; nothing on board, nothing out of place. As he had turned to go, the boat with the detectives appeared on the other side of the bay. It was a few miles away, but he was sure it was them. He pulled his binoculars out and brought them into focus. Just as fast as they appeared; they disappeared, coming back to this side of the bay.

It piqued his curiosity for a moment. He was sure they weren't looking for the same thing he was looking for. Next trip to the sheriff's office he would ask. It never hurt to keep up with the locals; and he could use another reason to feast his eyes on detective Dupree.

* * * * *

The murder book was growing, of course, not as fast as Willa hoped. The new entries left a lot of speculation. The autopsy was in, no surprise there. The body would be released to the family today. In Willa's mind the only way she could express her condolences was by solving this; giving the family closure. She still had a long way to go; and it pained her. The mobile home was still a crime scene, but they had gathered evidence that was being sifted through. Luther's finances were one. He had been an investment broker; it seemed a very successful one, by the value of his accounts.

* * * * *

Earl hadn't shaved since he arrived. He was beginning to like this scruffy look. He had bought shorts and t-shirts and was trying hard to become a local. He didn't want to stand out in a crowd.

He had parked at the 7-11 just north of Big Bart's, waiting for Silas to finish up there and head to their meeting place. He would follow him to Lonnie's, a place where they weren't likely to run into any of the regulars from Bart's. He was patting himself on the back for hiring Silas, who was turning out to be just what he needed. Silas had a great reputation and that was what had clinched the deal. Now he knew he would be helpful in ways he never thought necessary. Silas' car left the parking lot traveling fast. Earl pulled out just as fast.

He wasn't far behind, but Silas was already out of his car and walking to the door when Earl pulled into a parking space. He sat for a minute surveying the area. Lonnie's was off 301 in a neighborhood that probably had been considered affluent many years ago. The homes were larger but not so well kept. This area would have been part of a better class.

Lonnie's itself had a small neon sign in the large front window. The window was shaded inside with blinds that did not allow anyone in the parking lot to see what was going on inside. The parking lot was well-lit with several prominent security cameras to protect the customers. Earl walked the short distance to the door, a large leather covered double door that instructed you to 'use this door'; as the other half of the double door was locked.

The noise level was low, and no one stopped what they were doing to check him out. That is, no one except Lonnie. Silas was standing at the end of the bar talking to her. She must have clued him in to the new customer, because he immediately turned toward the door.

Smiling, he turned back to Lonnie and nodded. She walked away as he headed over to Earl. "Hey man, you made good time," he said with a large smile on his face.

"Yeah, you were easy to follow. Let's have a drink."

The place wasn't crowded so they had their choice of seats and chose a small table in the back corner. Lonnie came over to the table to take their order. "Lonnie, this is a friend of mine from Chicago. Meet Earl Brookfield. Earl, Lonnie, owner and local informational news source."

Earl stood up, stuck out his hand. "Good to meet you."

"Just because I know everything, doesn't mean I tell everything," she laughed. She had an easy laugh, and a friendly demeanor that Earl immediately liked.

When she left to get their drinks Silas said, "She has a bartender that does this. She just came over to meet you."

"That's good. I like that," he answered.

"Next time you come in here she will remember what you are drinking and anything else she learned about you."

"Thanks for the heads up," Earl said thinking, I like this place already. It reminded him of home.

Lonnie placed their drinks on the table without another word and walked away. Silas had a lot to report; most of it didn't point Earl in the direction he was looking for. "No one is talking about Cole. At all. Bart has already removed all signs of him. Meaning, a picture of him and his boat; a boat he bought from Bart a few years ago."

"Interesting," Earl was trying to wrap his mind around this when Silas told him, "Don't look now, but local law enforcement just came through the door."

Of course, that made his head swivel. "Do they come here often?"

"Oh yes, this is their favorite hangout. Lonnie and Detective Dupree seem to be good friends."

"That's good to know!"

Willa, Russell, and Frank ordered their drinks at the bar. After a few minutes they headed to the tables near the rear of the room. Willa had noticed Silas as she entered but didn't recognize the broad-shouldered man sitting with his back to her. Then it dawned on her; the first time she had seen him he was in his expensive sport coat and his Gucci shoes. He looked darn good in a T-shirt, shorts, and sandals.

The two men quit talking as the detectives approached. "Hey Silas, Earl, good to see you took my advice. You can't find a better local than Silas." Willa said.

Earl smiled.

"Thanks for the business, Willa. I owe you," Silas said.

"Yes, you do!" Willa grinned.

The detectives came to Lonnie's often after work. Although it wasn't a real cop bar; not like some might think. Anyone was welcome here. However, the appearance of the law, in uniform or not, kept the lawless out and made for a comfortable place to relax.

Silas and Earl were not so single-minded that they didn't wonder, what, if anything, was going on with the detectives. The detectives were talking in very animated voices, but in hushed tones to avoid being overheard. Earl knew he wasn't leaving here without having a word with Detective Willa Dupree.

Chapter 17

The phone vibrated in the back pocket of his faded blue jeans, he glanced around the room, a shiver ran through his body. Only one person had the number to this phone. "Yeah?" he answered, keeping his voice low, as he walked outside. The stars were bright, and the moon was visible; the forecast was for rain tonight but right now it appeared as if it wasn't happening any time soon.

"We need to meet! Tonight! Twelve o'clock!" the voice was marked with seriousness and the message far outweighed the few words necessary to relay it.

"Same place?"

"Yes."

"I'll be there!"

As those words left his lips, his caller hung up and he was listening to a dial tone. Sweat started to cover his forehead. He had been afraid this call would come. Well, he could handle it; he could handle anything. He didn't want to dwell on the reasons. And he was sure things were not beyond simple reasoning, a meeting to settle the nerves of his cousin would do the job. Things were not that bad, yet.

* * * * *

Driving to Duette late at night was totally different than the same drive during the day time. Just once, he'd like to be taking this trip for the pleasure of it. As he passed Parrish he smiled. Nice well-lit highway, not many people out this time of night, traffic was light. Parrish was a small town that continued to grow. It seemed all previously undeveloped acreage now had new and well-built communities cropping up. Where there had once been a small-town diner, Pizza Hut had a taken over. Even though it was closed at this hour, the strip mall boasted a Publix, a garage and a variety of small businesses. Highway 301 cut right through the middle of town, but he wasn't slowing down. A right turn at State Road 62 and how things could change. No street lights, no houses, only farms.

Growing up here he hated it, couldn't wait to leave town. Now here he was, back again. As it was 45 to 50 miles from Sarasota and had less traffic than any other town around; it was designated as the perfect spot to meet. The fact that it was known as 'off the beaten path' made it the place for these meetings. The stress of the situation made the drive seem like it went on forever. The moon was now hidden behind clouds and the forecasted rain looked imminent. As the place came into view, he slowed and was almost tempted to pass it by; but thought better of it and turned in as expected.

It was just a shell drive with grassy parking spaces along the right. The one-teacher elementary school still had a flag on the pole, blowing in the breeze. The only light on the property was the lone spotlight pointed upward to illuminate the American flag. He remembered his school job in fifth and sixth grades, raising the flag each morning. It was the highlight of the day, classes after that were a drag. He was the biggest kid in class even before he failed a grade. Miss Lewis didn't know how to cope with a boy taller than she was; bigger in every way. She gave it her best, but he refused to accept any help. If it wasn't for social passing he could still be here. Well, not really. This school recently closed for good. The last one-teacher elementary school in Florida; lack of students and lack of funding. He almost chuckled remembering that night so long ago, slipping out late and exchanging the American flag for a Confederate one after receiving a failing grade in history. He thought that would show them. He didn't get caught, but it caused a rift between the school and the board of education.

School always came easy for his cousin. That was why he resented him so much. And the reason he finally left Duette and headed to Sarasota. As luck would have it, his cousin also moved to Sarasota after graduating from the University of Florida. They had nothing in common and ran in totally different circles, until they needed each other.

His cousin had been very helpful in securing the license for opening his business. A business that was not dependent on tourists. A business he would have been unable to acquire without his cousin's help. But, his cousin didn't help him out of the goodness of his heart. The cost made him in debt forever to his cousin. As a result, he was always having to make 'problems' go away. That bound the two together in ways he would have never imagined.

Tonight, he didn't have a clear idea as to how to handle this small bump in the road. He would let his cousin lead the way; that's the way it always went. He could see headlights of a coming vehicle and he knew it would be him. He wiped the sweat from his eyes and opened his truck door. The only other vehicle on the road pulled in beside him.

Before he could drag his tired body into his cousin's car, his cousin was already saying, "Ok, tell me about that old guy! Is it connected?"

He hesitated; he had to get this right. "He was a loose cannon, a possible witness. He could have seen enough to make waves. He was old, he was expendable."

"You had better hope there is no connection made by the police."

"Wait a minute. Who do you think you are? Are you threatening me? Because that would not turn out well for you."

Backing down a little, his cousin said, "I'm just saying, can we fix this? Do we need to fix it?"

"We fixed it! Period! You don't have anything to worry about. Your job is safe; I'm sure that's what your concern is."

His cousin smiled, "I knew you were good for this." Reaching over for the first time, he patted his cousin on the shoulder. "By the way, how's business?"

"Business is fine; you know I don't depend on the same people you do for a living."

"Yeah, I almost forgot."

"Anything else?"

"No, that's it."

He pushed open the door of the late model car as rain started to fall. After staring at the flag for a moment, he climbed into his own vehicle, never glancing at his cousin as he pulled out of the old school parking lot. He hit the windshield wipers and hoped he wouldn't be returning anytime soon.

Barbara Marvin

Chapter 18

Willa was in the office early. She felt the pressure of this case heavy on her shoulders. There was something about this that left an uncomfortable void; something missing, and not just evidence. In her mind, she couldn't push aside a feeling that they had it all wrong. This wasn't what it seemed and frankly, if they weren't very careful this could end up in the cold case file.

Cap had insisted they all be in early. She knew they would, even if he had not demanded it. She looked around, everyone was here except Cap. His door was closed, but the large picture window that was meant to give transparency to the office, also gave her a view of his desk. No Cap.

"Russ, what time did you get in?" she asked, motioning to Caps office.

"Not long before you, Kevin? Frank? How about you guys?" Russ queried.

"I've been here about an hour," Kevin replied. "Cap was here and went tearing out ten minutes after I got here. I don't think he even saw me. I was making coffee. Somebody has to do it," he joked.

The emotion passing through Willa stunned her, she wondered if this was about her. Shaking it off, she stood up. "Let's see what we have; let's put everything together."

"I've hit a dead end with the DIL. Their number goes straight to voice mail with a recorded message asking you to leave your number and someone will get back to you. So far, nothing. No return calls." Frank said. Frank had also done a search for similar cases in the area. Nothing stood out.

Nothing in Luther's background had looked out of place. At first glance, he was just another displaced Yankee. Sarasota was full of them. Although he seemed to be well-off financially, he wasn't very social. Nothing in his home indicated he ever went to local theaters, concerts, or other entertainment venues. McDonald's for coffee seemed to be the extent of his social activities, with an occasional fishing trip with one of the guys.

Willa was not herself; not the confident detective she had become. The lack of progress was getting to her. Something about the facts was bothering her, something she couldn't put her finger on. They were missing a very crucial part of the puzzle. Why would someone put a hit out on a man who had few friends and no known enemies? The friends he had were just as unconnected to the criminal element in town as Luther was. The exception might be retired detective Vassar and she needed to talk to him again. "Kevin," she said. "Call your dad, ask him to come in again; I need to talk to him."

"Okay. He'll be glad to hear that. You know he wants to insert himself in this." Kevin replied.

"Good, maybe his experience and his friendship with Landrow can help." Willa respected experience, age, and knowledge. She was stumped, might as well take advantage of any help Kevin's dad might have to offer, even if she usually didn't feel like he should be involved in law enforcement efforts. This was different.

* * * * *

Jon was busy, deadlines to meet, interviews to complete and on top of all this, he wanted to see Earl. No one in his office knew he was as involved with Cole as he was, no one knew about Earl and for the time being, he was going to keep it that way. Earl had plenty to report, so he set up a meeting; Lonnie's was the place.

Jon had wanted Marina Bar on the beach, but Earl was already becoming comfortable with this town. Maybe comfortable is the wrong word, he was aware of where he was welcome and where he wasn't. And, he knew where he wanted to go. When Jon walked in, Earl was at the bar; in a conversation with no other than the owner. To say Earl looked at home was putting it mildly.

"Jon, over here!" Earl said.

Jon nodded. "I see you, how are you?"

"Fine,." he replied after glancing at Lonnie. "Let's sit at a table."

Jon smiled at Lonnie and ordered a beer as they moved to the back of the room. They sat at the same table as before; Jon was feeling a pattern here. Sometimes routines were an advantage, he hoped this one was. Earl looked very comfortable as he opened his notebook.

*   *   *   *   *

Willa got home late. Not unusual when the office was busy. She grabbed a bottle of water from the fridge and walked out on the lanai. The beach was deserted at this time of night. The waves continued to roll in, making a muffled sound. The sky was cloudless, and she could see several bright stars. She wondered why she couldn't recall their names; she knew she had learned them in school as a child.

She had spent many nights sitting in the dark outside her parent's home concentrating on the stars. It had helped her shut out the sounds of her father as he abused and berated her mother on a regular basis. Dinner wasn't hot enough or served soon enough or why wasn't there dessert. Who ate it? She continually shut these sounds out; never wanting to go inside.

After her father had quieted down, she knew he had drunk himself into a stupor and had probably fallen asleep on the ratty old sofa. She would wait a few more minutes and then slip in the back door and walk to her bedroom. Each night she prayed that her father wouldn't wake up in the morning. That she and her mother would be free; and then she prayed that God would forgive her these terrible thoughts.

Tonight, she had no such thoughts. Tonight, she had a job to do. She had promised Luther's son she would find closure for his pain. Just like the past; there were no answers in the stars. She turned and went back inside.

Chapter 19

Sarasota Bay was a beautiful place. Of course, most ads and alluring tourist commercials were taken during the day when the warm sunlight glistened on the still blue waters. This morning, before sunup, there wasn't any glistening and no still water. As a matter of fact, there was no one out here except one boat with two middle aged commercial fishermen expecting to catch mullet and then transport them to the closest fish house. Along with overpopulation, often comes contamination of local waters. Although Sarasota had grown exponentially, the bays were not on the "do not eat fish from these waters" list, yet.

The oyster beds that had provided income for these fishermen in the past; were now few and far between. A lot of these delicate appetizers on the menu at local restaurants were now being imported from other locations. However, even with dwindling availability, commercial fishing was still a vocation for a few.

The storm that blew in last night didn't dampen the outlook of these locals. They considered it normal weather, hoping to finish and by home before the tourist got in the way. As daybreak approached, the tourists begin to fill these waters. The fishermen took their usual route out into the gulf in their small, beat-up skiff. They managed to catch enough to eke out a living most weeks. They had their own opinion about the controversial law passed over twenty years ago concerning the size of the nets allowed to catch certain fish. Since the use of large seine nets had been outlawed, the brothers had gotten very good at throwing the circular cast nets. Mullet tend to jump out of the water periodically, making them easy to spot. Jake killed the motor and let the boat drift. He was looking at the movement in the dark water, pointing out to

Kyle an area that just might be the first haul of the day.

Kyle threw the net; it opened perfectly and dropped quickly over the rough water. Pulling the lead rope that allowed him to control it caused the net to form, trapping, what he hoped would be a good catch. The brothers didn't converse much while they were working, so when Jake said, "Hey Kyle, I think we caught a boat full," Kyle quickly looked to the net Jake was dragging toward the boat.

"Yeah?" questioned Kyle.

"Yes!" said Jake feeling the weight of the net as he turned his head and looked at Kyle.

"What the hell did you catch?" demanded Kyle staring at the net!

* * * * *

The ambulance and several other emergency vehicles arriving at the municipal pier, caused the area to become packed with spectators. Local law enforcement immediately started directing traffic away from the scene.

Willa got the call as she was heading to the office and changed direction immediately. When she arrived, she parked and caught up with Russell, who obviously had gotten the same call. "What's up?" she asked him.

"Those fishermen" he said, pointing to the end of the pier, "found a body in the gulf just a short time ago."

Today is off to a bad start, she thought. Glancing around, she noticed a crowd already gathering. "Boy… it doesn't take long to draw a mob."

"No, it doesn't," Russell answered under his breath.

At the end of the pier, two men were talking to local authorities, both looked ragged. She didn't know if the circumstances had an influence on that or if that was their usual appearance. Their body language suggested they wanted to be anywhere but here.

From his high-rise apartment across the street, Jon could see the commotion at the pier. The ambulances, squad cars and several other law enforcement vehicles had arrived with lights flashing, but no sirens. He skipped his shower and threw on his clothes. He called his camera man on the way to the scene. He had no idea what was going on or if it was important, but he would get the story and worry about that later.

The blue tarp that had been carefully bound around the body was now in tatters. The gulf was full of predatory fish and they had done their job trying to get at the contents. There was evidence of that on the upper torso. Before covering the body with the large medical sheet, Willa searched the pockets of the blue jeans and located a wallet.

Since the boat wasn't the crime scene, nor was the pier, Willa had the EMT's move the body to the waiting stretcher, preparing it for immediate removal to coroner's office. She motioned for the body to be wheeled to the waiting vehicle. Jon's cameraman caught it all, even if no one was answering any of his questions.

This was the second time in as many days that Willa had contact with a boat. She felt a little seasick but managed to keep her breakfast down, as the small skiff rocked back and forth. Even before she found the wallet on the victim, she was sure who she was looking at. Her gaze automatically moved east to the beautiful high rise, the home of Jon Albee and then to Jon himself, as she noticed he was already here.

As of now, Jon's friend, Cole Mitchell was no longer missing.

Chapter 20

Back at headquarters, Kyle and Jake were being interviewed in separate rooms. Both men were visibly shaken; they had nothing that would help the detectives. After about an hour they were allowed to leave with instructions not to leave town.

Willa, Russell, and Kevin gathered at the coffee pot. Willa really wanted Starbucks, but that would have to be put on hold. Right now, she didn't even have time to walk across the street. "We will have to wait for the autopsy," she said. "However, the bruising and discoloration on the neck is most likely strangulation."

"Yes, that's what it looked like to me," Russell added. "This is only the second time I've seen a body recovered from the gulf.

Those fish did a job on him. We are lucky he wasn't out there longer," he said, with the vision of Cole's body fresh in his mind.

It was a rough day, now they had not one, but two murders. Their work load had just doubled.

* * * * *

After finally calling it a day, Willa left the office late. Her drive home contained mental images she tried to erase. She was home before she knew it and still couldn't turn off her inner thoughts.

Spent from a day filled with one hurdle after another, she was glad to hear the calming roar of the surf; on a normal day this was what she looked forward to. She would have trouble sleeping tonight. She contemplated the sleeping pills in the bathroom; but not tonight. Even though her doctor assured her they would help. She had learned long ago, her nights and days were not her own; she must be able to wake up and be alert at a moment's notice. She had filled the prescription but had not taken the medication because of these requirements of the job.

It was midnight when she turned off the bedroom light. Her notes and memos were neatly stacked on the bedside table. Standing in front of the west window, she appreciated the sounds, thundering along, as if they were saying, "I'm angry; look at me! What happened to Cole? Look at me! What do you see? I gave him back to you. Find out what happened!" She continued to stare as far as she could see; nothing. The surf roared, and the moon like a thief, hid behind the clouds.

Over the years, she often pulled up a chair and sat here for hours looking at the vast scene in front of her. Five years ago, after her dad had passed away, she sat here as she worried about not feeling sad. Maybe gratitude; maybe relief, but not sorrow. She finally learned she was bigger than the emotions; she was strong. Choosing to pursue law enforcement, she was determined she would be a driving force for innocent victims. And she was. Sarasota was the place she chose to do that after living in Atlanta for years.

Sometimes we take for granted things close to us. We bury our heads in the sand. She was no longer that little girl. She was a woman. A woman empowered by knowledge, education, and she hoped someday, self-esteem. She could never be anything else.

Maybe she could sleep now. She closed the blinds and sat on the bed. The short prayer she said was not about herself, but for finding the terrible person responsible for Luther Landrow's demise and the gruesome murder of Cole, that the fishermen had just discovered.

Somehow, she felt calmer as she laid her head on her pillow. She had no answers but if possible, she would find them. Tomorrow.

The calm didn't last long. She was reliving the scenes of today, playing back all she knew. Tossing and turning, she punched her pillow. No help. Maybe a glass of water; as she threw back the sheets, she rose and stood by the bed. The moonlight was peeking through the blinds, she walked to the window, opened it just a bit. She let out a quick gasp; as her over stimulated mind 'saw' someone standing on the beach looking up at her house. She looked again, and it was not her imagination. Sure enough, a man in dark clothing stood still for a moment, then turned and left the beach walking south.

"Who is that?" she thought, the water was forgotten. Sleep would have to wait.

Barbara Marvin

Chapter 21

Jon called his father in Chicago to fill him in. It was the worst call of his life. After a moment of silence, his dad wanted to come down for a while. "That won't be necessary, but thanks anyway," he said. "But would it be possible to keep Earl here a little longer? I need him more than ever."

"He's yours... as long as it takes."

"Thanks again dad. When this is solved, I'll come home. I'll need a break."

"Jon, is there anything else? Whatever you need; you know I'm here for you," his father became very emotional and Jon could hear it in his voice. This was a man who was normally unemotional. Jon was moved by it.

"Thanks Dad...I love you. Bye!" he ended the call and closed his eyes. What reason would anyone have for killing his friend?

He knew the investigation needed to kick into high gear.

* * * * *

Willa's drive home was getting later and later; it was hard to get out the door with the hectic pace in the office trying to deal with two major cases. As she hit the garage door opener, the motion detector lights in the driveway and in the garage came on. She slammed on the brakes, stopping quickly before pulling any further into the drive.

The light cast a shimmer on something dark red and wet, spread in front of her. It was a puddle, maybe two feet across. "What is in my driveway," she blurted out loud.

As she jumped out of her car, she looked around. No one was in sight. She quickly slipped her gun out of its holster and held it at her side. Her first thought was, "whose blood is that?"

She neared the puddle, squatted down and touched it with her finger tip, bringing it to her nose. "Paint... red paint," she muttered disgustedly. She moved back to her car and called Russell. She remained in her car for the fifteen minutes it took Russ to arrive. She then stepped out, shaking her head as he opened his car door. "Thanks for coming, Russ."

"You sounded upset" he replied. "How could I not?"

"I am, someone deliberately poured paint on my driveway and expected me to think it was blood, which I did. Look at this"

"Well, I'm making a report. We'll start there. Can you think of anyone who might do this? Anyone mad at you? Why your driveway?" Russell was taking pictures of the spot with his phone, as he questioned her.

It took a whole roll of paper towels to soak up the paint. Willa had put on rubber gloves and worked diligently. After it was up, all that was left was the big red stain to remind her. Tomorrow she would see what she could do about that.

She and Russell entered the kitchen after pulling their cars into the garage and lowering the door. He made sure she had calmed down and hoped she could sleep tonight. He offered to spend the night to make her feel safer.

"Thanks, but I'll be ok," she said.

Long after he had left, she was standing all alone in the kitchen; turning out the lights, she glanced out the window and then headed upstairs. Her shoulders ached, her head hurt, and she knew it would be a rough night. Why were all these things happening now? She needed to get back to her normal routine. She tried to remember what normal was. The gulf had calmed, but her mind was stilling spinning through the events of the last few days.

She put on her pajamas and turned off the light before she walked to the window. As she looked over the water a picture came racing back to her. The picture from last night, the man on the beach. Why was he there? Did it have anything to do with this mess tonight? Shaking her head, she closed the blinds, no crack left to allow the moon light in. No physical distractions to interfere with sleep tonight.

When she woke the next morning, she was surprised she had slept through the night. It was getting light out and the gulf was loud, but not so loud that she wanted to shut it out. Loud enough to remind her of the last two nights. Now she was anxious to get to work trying to make some sense of everything that was happening.

Some days, Willa sipped coffee as she looked out and reflected on her job, her life, her accomplishments. Today she wanted to forget about her life, forget about last night. Focus on Cole, his life, his job, his accomplishments.

As she took a seat at Cap's morning meeting, the atmosphere was sober, even Russell appeared quieter than usual. After rehashing all the info, they had about Cole, they were ready to disband. "Wait just a minute… last night Willa had a surprise," Russell glanced at her. "Tell them about your visitor, Willa."

"I don't think this has anything to do with what we are working on," she shrugged but continued. "When I pulled into my drive last night, there was a big puddle of red paint in front of my garage. Luckily, I saw it and didn't drive through it, because I could have had a huge mess. Bigger than I had." She looked around the table, "I don't know who I pissed off, but there it was."

Cap looked up sharply. "Did you see anyone, was there any other indication that someone was there?"

"That was all I saw, I cleaned it up. But, I'm pretty mad." Willa replied. Russ passed his phone around the table with the picture. "If you guys hear anything, let me know. Otherwise, I'm going to try to ignore it for now." She shut her notebook, closing the discussion.

Chapter 22

When he read the headline, he couldn't believe his eyes. His first thought was for himself. What price would he pay for this? What could he do to prevent the backlash he knew would happen if this wasn't handled properly? This would not be a normal day; he headed to the medicine cabinet.

The aspirin bottle was half full; he poured two in his hand, thought about it and shook out two more. Four probably wouldn't help. He looked at the bottle. Not enough to put him out of his misery. He quickly tossed the handful in his mouth, followed by several gulps of water.

Wiping the dripping water from his mouth and chin, he looked at himself in the mirror. The usual scowl was there, the cold brown eyes were there, the unkempt straggly hair was there. He always managed to alter that look each morning.

He smiled as he contemplated a solution to his problem. Only one thing would protect him. Was he man enough to do it or was he just the one giving orders? He had so much to lose, either way. Turning to the mirror, that phony photo opt expression that worked so well in the past would have to do.

Another cup of coffee, caffeine was a necessity.

Rereading the article, he studied every word, focusing on the journalist. Jon Albee seemed to be everywhere. Not that smart, not a long-time resident. He recalled his first encounter with him. Jon was trying hard to make a name for himself and was willing to do most anything to forward his own agenda. These young people have no standards today. Jon would be easy to influence. He stored that thought in the back of his mind, as he finished prepping for his day.

* * * * *

The detectives refused to meet with Earl, but they knew he wasn't going away. However, given the current situation they had no time now; things had changed. Lisa, as usual had them covered. She talked to Jon and had him break the news to Earl, along with a promise to see him real soon. Earl understood, he had a plan in mind already, one he could implement without their interference. This wasn't his first rodeo.

The round table meeting in Cap's office convened as soon as everyone was in. Captain Dunbar was under more pressure than ever, with two homicides, his appearance showed it. Willa was sure it wasn't the only reason. Feedback from his superiors and the politics of the office were taking a toll on him. The bags under his eyes grew every day. She couldn't remember seeing him this bad.

The talk was loud and non-stop. Everyone filled him in on what was happening; it went downhill from there. When Cap started to speak, his voice was slow, his tone very measured. Willa looked twice to make sure it was Cap. He had always been good at raising his voice; he seemed to think yelling helped get his point across. Not today.

They filled him in on the trip to Cole's apartment. It was now part of a criminal investigation and sealed off. His phone and computer had been recovered. Willa remembered Jon saying Cole had received a death threat. At the time Cole didn't believe him, didn't take it seriously, now they needed to find out more.

Frank was on it. If it came from a phone call, they might be able to trace it. Life was never predictable; just when things were looking up...well, Cole was a perfect example. His book was published, he was recognized as an up and coming author, and he thought he might get his life back on track and then "boom."

After the meeting, which lasted less than an hour, Willa passed out copies of Cole's book. "Read this... if you have time. Don't know if it contains anything we can use, but you never know," she stated.

Chapter 23

Willa enjoyed hard work; it proved to her she was important. The harder she worked the more meaning her life had. She had used this philosophy since she became an adult.

It had put her at the top of the class in college, even though she always had two jobs in college as she needed to provide for herself. She had received several grants and loans during this time. Living extravagant never crossed her mind. Now she was making a good salary but there were still more rungs on the ladder and she anticipated the climb.

After a long day in the office, she left the building and headed north. A short stop at Lonnie's Bar was looking pretty good right now. As she pulled into the well-lit parking lot at Lonnie's, she smiled to herself. Lonnie was always there for her. To listen or to advise. Tonight, she needed to relax and then get some much-needed sleep. As she slammed the car door she heard, "Ms. Dupree. Detective Dupree."

A well-dressed middle-aged man was quickly approaching her vehicle. The hair on the back of her neck stood up, her hand automatically went to her revolver. "Yes," she answered, staring him down.

The man was smiling, about six feet tall, well shaven, casually dressed like a business man and holding out his hand. "My name is Paul Graves, I'm with Smith and Blackwell in Chicago. Could I speak with you for a moment?"

Willa ignored his hand and replied, "What can I do for you?"

Paul carefully reached into his breast pocket and retrieved a business card and held it out for her.

She ignored it and repeated, "What can I do for you?"

He turned and glanced at Lonnie's. "I have been sent here to offer you a job; we need people like you where I come from. Can I buy you a drink?"

She paused, and then replied, "I was just headed in, we can discuss it inside." They walked toward the door together. She took the business card and read it. A Chicago detective agency, wonder how they heard about me? She was a little flattered. Being from the Windy City, he probably didn't know that Lonnie's was a cop bar. Pure and simple. One of the safest places in the city. However, she wasn't about to tell him. Let him give her his pitch. When he left; she could relax.

Willa entered the door first, with Paul behind her. Lonnie looked up from her position behind the bar, getting a good view of both Willa and Paul. She smiled and was ready to welcome them, until she saw the look on Willa's face and her lips saying "shhhh." Willa was telling her to tone it down, play this by ear, treat them like two random customers. So that's what she would do.

Willa led Paul to a table in the back, pulled out a chair facing the door, thereby letting Paul face the rear of the room. Lonnie walked over, placed coasters on the table. "What can I get for you two tonight?"

Willa ordered vodka and tonic, Paul ordered a draft beer.

"I'll be right back with that," Lonnie offered, looking Willa in the eye. Lonnie knew something was up. Willa did not elaborate; so she would wait and see.

Paul began his sales pitch immediately. "Let me tell you a little about our company, Smith and Blackwell. We are an unknown in the public world; but well known in the professional world. Our office is downtown, and we are quite busy. We are always looking for top-notch employees. I'm not sure how we got your name; but let me say, your reputation precedes you."

He paused and looked deep into Willa's eyes, she just returned the gaze without offering a reply. He took a swallow of beer, smiled, and continued to impress her with his knowledge of her professional life. "How does this sound to you? Would you be interested in hearing more?"

"I have to tell you, I'm happy where I am. I am not looking for another job."

"All the more reason to listen to me. We love people that are working hard, not bad mouthing their current employer. Not looking to move; on the other hand, our company is looking for the best."

Willa's mind was in overdrive. If Paul was judging her interest in him by the look on her face, he had her. In actuality, she was a good detective; part of her success in this field was due to her intuition. Right now, she couldn't miss the red flags. Staring into his face she was focused on why he was here, why he was pursuing her, and who was he. She didn't for a minute believe he was here to recruit her for the job he was playing up; but the salary would be hard to resist. Until she knew the real story, she would keep him interested in her.

They continued to talk, she signaled Lonnie for another round of drinks. Lonnie did her job and didn't interfere in this private conversation. After finishing the second drink, Willa smiled. "I like your offer; can I think about it?"

"Of course," Paul said with a grin, "but I will need an answer soon. We do have other applicants in mind, and I have to get back to

Chicago. Can you let me know by tomorrow sometime?"

"Yes, I think that will work for me."

They both stood at the same time, he held out his hand and this time she shook it. "Suppose we meet here tomorrow night, say, same time," he suggested.

"Sounds good to me," she declared.

He threw forty dollars on the table, much more than their bar bill. "Can I walk you to your car?" he asked.

"Thanks, but I need to visit the ladies room before I go. I'll see you tomorrow," she said dismissing him as she turned toward to back of the room.

Lonnie, who was alert to Willa and her conversation, had sent her other bartender outside to smoke before Paul left the building. His instructions were, get a picture of the car and the man. She didn't know if it would be useful or not, but Willa could thank her later if it was helpful.

Willa spent enough time in the bathroom to allow Paul to leave. Then, she walked directly to the bar and face to face with Lonnie. "What was that all about?" Lonnie questioned.

"Beats me, did you see him leave? What was he driving?"

"Jimmie," Lonnie grinned, "I got you covered. What do you have there, Jimmie?"

Willa looked at Lonnie and then at Jimmie. "You should be a detective!" she said as Jimmie handed her his phone with the very clear picture of Paul and his car.

"I am a detective; how do you think I can run this bar and stay out of trouble," she laughed.

Willa had Jimmy send the pictures to her phone; she shook her head and said, "I'm tired, I'm heading for home, I'll fill you in later after I do a little research myself. Thanks for jumping in like you did. He will be back tomorrow night and so will I."

As she left, she felt another sleepless night coming on.

Barbara Marvin

Chapter 24

After the early morning meeting, Captain Dunbar left the office rather abruptly.

Willa had not mentioned to anyone her encounter with Paul Graves last night. She would complete her research and then share it with Russell. Right now, it was distracting her from her job. And … she felt that was exactly what it was supposed to do.

Someone on the beach checking out her house, someone pouring paint on her driveway, someone offering her a job. Not just a job, but one in another state. Her mind tried to find a reason; tried to find some connection. She wasn't getting close to solving the first case; were the events connected to the case? Now, she was dealing with two cases; were the cases related? Were the events related to the cases? Could she be closer than she thought? Not likely she thought as she opened her desk drawer and found the business card she was looking for.

"Hello Detective Dupree, so nice of you to call me," Earl sounded surprised to hear from her.

"Hello Earl," Willa answered. "I'll get right to the point of this call. Could you come by the office this morning?"

"I guess so, do you mind telling me why?"

"I have a few questions I'd like to run by you."

"We could do it over lunch or dinner," he bantered.

"No, we couldn't. But thanks anyway."

"What time do you need me," he said smiling to himself. He would stop everything now if it would make her happy.

"As soon as possible. I'll be here all morning. Just stop by when it is convenient; I'll alert the receptionist."

"Ok, will do,"

"Thanks Earl, see you soon," Willa hung up and even smiled to herself. With Cap out of the office, she felt ok about bringing Earl in under false pretenses. She noticed Russell watching her. She would have to tell him sooner or later. Now might be the right time.

She tried filling Russ in on what she knew and what she didn't know. And why she was having Earl come in, but he was a little confused. She hadn't told him everything. Was someone trying to get rid of her? Get her out of town? Or was she totally reading this all wrong?

Waiting for Earl to arrive gave Willa time to finish her research on Smith and Blackwell of Chicago and Paul Graves, if that was his real name. She was impressed with the company's reputation. Paul Graves was another matter. She couldn't find anything relating to him. It made her think he wasn't who he said he was. That was ok, she intended to play his little game. At least until she found out what was going on.

* * * * *

When Earl arrived, June ushered him into conference room two. It was smaller and more intimate. Willa needed to work this just right. Of course, she had the upper hand; this was her office, her meeting and most likely, her problem. Earl was dressed very casually. He was fitting right in. If Willa hadn't met him before, she would think he was a local. Fitting in was his game and he was good at it. As Willa shut the door, Earl stood up and held out his hand; she shook it. "Thanks for coming in, Earl. Good to see you."

"My pleasure," he replied.

"Are you making any headway, anything new on Cole Mitchell that you would like to share?" she asked.

"Nothing much. But I did see you and your team out on the water. I wondered what you found."

"Where were you?" this grabbed her attention.

"I was at Cole's boat."

"Where is that? We need to check it out," she said wondering how he got ahead of them on this.

"It's docked south of his apartment. You can check it. I already did. Nothing. Neat as a pin. Jon says that's the way he was about his boat."

After fifteen minutes Willa had all she could get from him about Cole and needed to get back to the real reason for this meeting. "On a different note," she started, "what do you know about a detective agency from Chicago named Smith and Blackwell? And a private eye named Paul Graves?"

"Are they involved in this? Are you working with them?" Earl seemed shocked for a moment.

Willa smiled, "I ask the questions."

"Oh yeah, for a minute I thought we might actually be sharing info," he quipped

"Funny, and yes we are sharing info. I just need to know about this group, and no they are not involved that I know of." For a minute

Willa thought she might have scared Earl off. She would be more careful in the future.

Earl grinned, "I've never worked with them. They are big in Chicago. I always felt they had some connections to the local government."

Willa nodded as she took notes.

Earl continued, "What is really going on? I may be new in Florida, but I didn't just fall off a turnip truck." Grinning ear to ear, this got a chuckle out of her.

She quickly changed her tone. "If you had any connections with that turnip truck, maybe I would tell you."

"Touché. Ok, let's start again. I'm sorry. I apologize for disrespecting your office. I would like nothing better than to work with you," he joked in mock contriteness.

"Good... now, where were we?" After a few more questions Willa got all she could from him. Paul Graves wasn't a name Earl recognized. She was drawing a blank on Graves, no matter where she checked. She wanted to leave it at that but felt uneasy not being able to get any thing on him. After all, tonight she would be seeing him again.

She hated feeling used. She hated not being ahead of the game. "Could I ask you for a favor, Earl?" Willa had a plan in mind.

As Earl departed the office, Willa felt a compulsory urge to share her distractions with Russ. She struggled with her inner feelings and knew Russ would help. She couldn't shut him out any longer. She had done that before and that hadn't work well.

Last year when her ex-husband was murdered she alienated Russ and the whole office; Captain Dunbar included. She was pulled off the case but refused to step back. After an unauthorized trip to Atlanta that no one here knew about, almost getting herself and others around her hurt, she was helpful in solving the case. It had taken months to be in the good graces of this office again.

The whole thing got off to a bad start, with Russell feeling unwanted and causing him to doubt her integrity. She promised Russell she wouldn't do that again...but here she was, on the brink. She closed her eyes, as if to block any more salacious thoughts.

Quickly opening them she saw Russell looking up expectantly at her. He didn't understand the expression on her face. After a few seconds, she motioned him to join her.

She preferred doing this in the privacy of a conference room, rather than be in the middle of an argument with him when Captain Dunbar walked in. Russell quietly rose and headed her way. "What's going on?" he asked as he stopped in front of her.

"Let's talk!"

* * * * *

Earl was a bit confused, but not for long. His first call was to his own office in Chicago; he assigned his partner back home a little work to do before tonight. Earl never entered a situation unprepared. Next, he called Samuel Albee. "Mr. Albee," Earl said as soon as he was connected with Sam.

"Yes, what's wrong? Is everything ok down there?" Sam had not expected to hear from Earl this early. Their pre-arranged phone meetings were scheduled later at night; after Earl had put in a full day's work.

"Yes … and no, I have a small dilemma, I need to share with you," Earl filled Samuel in on a fact that the sheriff's department had asked him to check out another detective agency in Chicago and since he was being paid by Sam, he wanted him to know. He also told him he wasn't sure it was tied to Cole's death, but he felt it was important to be considered an asset to the sheriff's department.

"Okay, do what you have too. Just keep me informed. And by the way, I'll see what I can do from here. I have a few connections myself that might help. You are right; it makes good business sense to get on the good side of the law."

"Thanks Sam. I'll be talking to you," Earl finished the call feeling better about what he was about to do. He wouldn't fill Jon in, just yet.

Barbara Marvin

Chapter 25

Jon was excited when Cole decided to write a novel; he promised to help all he could. He edited it and offered suggestions, made corrections and had been a big fan. One thing he never realized was, Cole had used a lot of actual facts. Facts that he was just now realizing were facts, he was using real crimes; and he was very accurate in the details. Jon never noticed until now that he was rewriting cold cases and calling them his own, calling them fiction, calling them his own book without saying they were based on cold cases. *The Murder Book* by Cole Mitchell.

He pulled the book from the shelf and opened it to the first gruesome scene. Taking the information given him by Lisa about a local business man, he began to compare the two. It seemed only the names had been changed; what had Cole done?

Jon sat back and closed his eyes. His friend never mentioned he was writing about an actual murder; one that happened right here. Jon recalled as he was going over the ending with Cole, he and Cole had differing opinions. Jon had suggested a little more sensationalism, a different bad guy. Cole was unwavering. He wouldn't change a thing. Now, Jon knew why. Cole wasn't writing fiction he was... what... just using real life, without any of his own ideas. Jon was disappointed in him. Nothing wrong with writing nonfiction, but he would at least expect Cole to say where he was getting the ideas from. As it was, it was published as if it were total fiction, a creative work of Cole's imagination. Clearly, it was not.

* * * * *

Kevin hesitated at Willa's desk as he headed for the coffee station. "Frank can't get a search warrant for the places on Siesta Key. No viable reason. We will have to go around it, I guess."

She nodded, her mind drifting from the information in front of her, to plans for this evening. Looking up, she flinched. She hadn't heard him. "Sorry, what did you say?"

"I'm working on a way to see those buildings on the Key. They don't appear to be occupied, can't be sure. Maybe they're for sale. I'll find a realtor. We could use that as a ploy. At least get an inside look. What do you say?"

"Good idea, Kevin. Keep looking."

Willa turned her attention to Frank. "Hey Frank. Did you learn anything about the Delaware owners?"

"Yes, a little. I'm still checking. Want to sit down and go over what I have?"

"Yeah, that sounds good. How about right after lunch?"

If things didn't keep moving forward, cases often stalled for years. Captain Dunbar was not up for more cold cases. His reputation was at stake, or at least he thought it was. He had not been successful in pushing for a new department to handle the cold cases.

Today, at the meeting with higher ups, he would push again. He had heard through the grapevine that the Mayor would be sitting in on the next meeting with the higher ups. He was torn about this, would it help or hurt his case? He would soon find out.

Mayor Sidney Sullivan would like to think this town was his town and he wanted to think it was crime free. So anytime something happened that might give it a bad name, he wanted it gone. He didn't care how, which irked Dunbar. Dunbar would use this to his advantage in getting new and larger monetary commitments this year. How can we keep crime down when we have to cut corners in law enforcement?

In the meantime, he would take the punches and protect his department.

* * * * *

Jon was not the only one feeling the necessity to read Cole's book. Earl had drawn a parallel between the day the book was released to the public and the possible death threat. It was possible Cole was making that up, but not likely. Earl read the book with nothing slanting his perception.

He started by making an outline, later he
would go over it with Jon. Compare notes;
see what the two had in common. He needed
to get this done as he had a full day ahead of
him. He was looking forward to tonight and
being allowed an inside view of something
important in another aspect of this
community. Not to mention, an opportunity
to work with the best-looking detective he
had ever met.

* * * * *

Willa believed she had no private life. She
had deep seated issues that made it seem
normal. As she looked around her, she
wondered where she would be in five years
or maybe even tomorrow. This new job offer
was a way out. A move to Chicago wasn't out
of the question. If there was anyone out there
for her, maybe she could find him in
Chicago. With a population of almost three
million people, could there be someone for
her. The greater metropolitan area had
nearly ten million. She knew she could
become one of them. The offer was starting
to look good.

What? Was she crazy? She knew this was
more than an offer for a job. It was a ploy to

get her out of this town, and when she got to the Windy City would there be a job or a misunderstanding? She shook her head. But then again, she wondered if she was considering it was because she would like to run away from relationship problems here.

She needed to focus on this case, on both of these cases and forget about being sidetracked by personal relationships or job offers. Yet, she continued to wonder why would anyone try to disrupt this investigation? Who would try to disrupt this investigation? If she could answer those questions, she would be on her way to clearing her desk of two open cases. She was preparing a list of questions for Paul. Tonight she would become an actress. She needed to show she was interested. Interested enough to convince Paul to give her one more day to decide. One day may not be enough, but it was a start.

Russell left the office early. Willa had taken him into her confidence and now he had work to do. Willa felt a little deceptive not keeping Captain in the loop, but at this point she was protecting him. From what, she wasn't sure. In the end if they closed their cases, it would be a win for him. It would go a long way in helping him influence the committee to add needed funding to expand his personnel, showing the department's ability to solve cases with their hard work and determination.

Tonight was a big night.

Barbara Marvin

Chapter 26

Willa had agreed to meet Paul in the parking lot of Lonnie's. She hoped he didn't insist they go somewhere else. There were a few more cars than usual as she pulled in, just as she knew there would be. Looking around she didn't see Paul's rental car. She had arrived a little early for that reason. She needed to see him arrive.

He came alone, that was a good sign. She got out and straightened her jacket. She made it a point to wear her uniform, as she called it. Her black slacks and white blouse with her gray loose-fitting jacket. Tonight her Glock felt good at her side. She knew she wouldn't need it, but she still wanted it there.

She had remembered to touch up her make-up and comb her hair. She wanted him to feel she had done it for him. As she approached him, the smile on her face would light up any dark parking lot. As beautiful as she was, the smile was a greeting itself. Paul grinned at her, aware of her looks but unaware she could read him like a book.

They shook hands and walked in together.

Willa pointed to the same table they had occupied before; it was empty and far enough from other customers seated in the area that they could talk privately and not be heard. Lonnie was there as they sat; Willa with her back to the wall and Paul with his to the bar. Placing coasters on the table she asked, "Good evening, what can I get you?"

"I'll have vodka and tonic" Willa replied; letting Paul order his draft beer.

Lonnie returned shortly with their drinks and smiled as she placed them on the table, turned and left without another word.

"Well Paul, it's good to see you, again." Willa offered.

"Good to see you, too," he replied.

"I have a few questions, if you don't mind," she continued.

"Fire away. That's why I'm here."

"Okay, first I'll tell you, I did my research on Smith and Blackwell," she paused just long enough for him to nod. "I was impressed. I even did some research on Chicago. Other than the occasionally harsh winter weather, it looks like a great place to live."

"I would have been disappointed if you hadn't done your homework. As for the weather, you get used to it."

"I hope so. But, who are you? I couldn't find anything on you."

Paul nodded, "Good job! Let me tell you, who I am doesn't matter. Let's say I'm a recruiter. They pay me to sell their company. You'll be working with some of the best detectives in one of the best cities in the country, but not with me."

Willa smiled. This meeting was going exactly as she predicted.

"When would they want me to start?" she questioned.

"As soon as possible. They have several large cases pending and expect more in the very near future."

The conversation continued for some time. Willa had many questions. Paul was able to answer most of them without hesitation.

Which to Willa meant, he had done his homework. It showed her just how anxious they were to establish a connection with her. She told him that and could see he was feeling pretty good about the job he was doing.

After ordering another round of drinks, Willa needed to wrap this up. "Paul, I'm impressed, as you can tell. I'm surprised that a company this big would come all the way to Florida to fill a vacancy."

He interrupted her, "Your reputation precedes you!" and he laughed lightly. "I'm not in on how they learned about you or your reputation as a detective; I only know they want you."

Willa sat, trying to look stunned. All the while hoping her next words would help to keep him on the hook, "You know if I take this job, I would have to sell my house, not to mention, find a place up there. Also, I'm leading a serious investigation now. That might put it on hold. That couldn't be good." She could see a glimmer in his eyes; he was feeling like a winner already.

"The company could provide you with a condo, they have units downtown just for situations like this. You would be welcome there until you found something. Most times they are willing to purchase your current home and resell it to take some of the stress out of the relocation. They are willing to go all out. Sounds hard to beat. What do you say?"

"Wow. I've never been propositioned like this before. You know what I'm thinking? How could I pass up an opportunity like this?"

"Yes, that's what I would say...but, it's only good for a short time. Give me your answer and we can start to put it together."

"It sounds perfect, but, could you give me one more day. I have a few friends I'll need to inform. I don't want them to think I'm rushing into anything."

"Willa... the company needs an answer, now."

"If they really want me, one day won't be a deal breaker, will it?"

"Let me make a fast call," he frowned as he took out his phone.

Willa grinned and nodded her acceptance.

Paul tapped in the number without hesitation. Willa sat silently, sipping her drink. He had turned his back to her and was speaking quietly and after a very short conversion, he was done.

"Okay, tomorrow is it! If at that time you can't decide, the offer is off the table. And, let me say, I do this all the time for them, they are being very good to you. Anyone else and I would be on my way out of here."

"Thank you, I'll remember that," she declared.

Paul raised his hand and signaled for the check. "It seems like we have covered everything," he acknowledged.

"Yes, I think we have. I had better get home, I have a lot to do, especially if I am going to be headed north," she admitted.

After paying the check they left Lonnie's together, and said goodbye in the parking lot.

Willa had told the group she would leave with him and head for home. Just in case he followed her, she would go to the beach and then she would return. They had a lot to figure out tonight.

At the table, Lonnie removed the dirty glasses, and the hidden recording device, and a small sign in the window saying the premises had visual and auditory surveillance. She was glad to be part of this charade. She enjoyed helping a friend like Willa anytime she could. Earl had gotten there early and met Russell. They sat just far enough away that their conversations were like background noise. Their role was to be two locals, there for a night out. Their responsibility was to be there if things got out of hand.

By the time Willa returned, Russell and Earl had listened to the whole conversation. They were ready to discuss the next step. Earl had a few things to lay on the table and it seemed Willa and Russ were agreeing that should happen, now. After an hour of discussion, they all agreed to go home, get some rest and meet tomorrow morning at the office.

"Earl, why don't you meet us... say about 8:30. We should be through with our meeting with Captain Dunbar by then," Willa suggested.

"Okay, I can do that," he answered.

They all said good night to Lonnie and walked out. Tomorrow looked to be more than a new day, it might be a new beginning in these cases.

Chapter 27

Willa was exhausted as she pulled in her garage. A mental picture of blood on the driveway came flooding back. Immediately, she wasn't tired; she was alert. Quickly closing the garage door, she exited her car. It was late and unusually quiet; except for the resounding roar of the waves. Everything was as she had left it, glancing around she now began to relax.

Knowing sleep might be evasive, she picked up Cole's book as she headed upstairs. Russell had made a big issue of her being alone. He was concerned for her, but tonight she wanted no more distractions. After convincing him she would go right home and stay there he relented, letting her leave Lonnie's alone.

Lonnie had been great tonight. But then she always was. Willa remembered how they met. She and Russell were getting background information on an open case and he suggested they talk to Lonnie Oster. Willa assumed she was a person of interest. As they parked at the bar just north of the city, she took it all in. Clean parking lot, security cameras, lighting, good neighborhood. Then she noticed the name on the window. "Lonnie's?" she asked Russell.

"Yes, she owns this place; and if anyone knows anything about our victim it will be her," he replied.

Turned out, he was right. The case was a local business man, a very successful banker turned real estate mogul. He was well known and respected. The case eventually went cold, but Willa and Lonnie hit it off.

She smiled to herself as she reached the top of the stairs. Tonight had been strange. She got the idea that Paul's only job was to recruit her. The part she hadn't been able to figure out was why. What was the motive for the big push to get her to Chicago? What connection did Chicago have to here? To her? How would anyone in Chicago know about her? Willa wasn't a fool. As much as she would like to think she was that great and as hard as she worked, she knew there were plenty of others that were just as good. There is just no logical reason for strangers from Chicago to be recruiting her.

Like so many other nights, Willa didn't expect to fall asleep right away, especially with her computer in her lap. She laughed and stacked the pillows behind her back. Might as well be comfortable. The list of names was growing, now for the connection. She felt a surge of adrenaline. She was getting closer. For her, the longer the list, the more options to consider.

Tomorrow morning would be her "come to Jesus" meeting with Captain Dunbar. This southern phrase described it well. A time of polite ultimatums followed by less polite threats. Captain needed to know something wasn't right; and she was in the middle of it. Someone wanted to get rid of her. She was pretty sure it had everything to do with this case.

She already surmised when she refused the offer to move, her life would be in grave danger. In essence, her life was already in danger. Her house on the beach, paradise to anyone else, was first in the line of attack. She tried to focus on what she was seeing online, it was impossible.

She threw the comforter off her feet and stood up. Had she set her security alarm? Of course, she had, she never forgot that. She needed a remote, she thought as she headed downstairs with the lights off. She needed to go inside the garage to activate or check the control. Inside her kitchen cabinet she had another control for the video cameras outside. All were on.

Tomorrow she would call the security company and have the ability to control the system added to her computer. She relaxed, knowing everything was set and working. Upstairs she once again looked at her computer. Looking back at her was the answer she had been searching for.

* * * * *

Jon sat up in the middle of his bed. Why had he thought Cole had copied his crime scenes from a cold case file? Cole wrote this book before the detectives had turned over the files to anyone outside the office. His first call tomorrow would be to Lisa. He knew what the answer would be before he asked. Lisa had not given this information to Cole; as a matter of fact, he was pretty sure Lisa and Cole had never really met or talked.

Jon recalled Cole's words, "I sat in this very bar and listened to all the wild tales." Could that be the source? Could that be the answer? He needed to contact the detectives. One other thing that now rang true. Cole had said he received a death threat. Had he published a deep dark secret. One that had long reaching tentacles. How involved were the regulars at Big Bart's and which ones?

* * * * *

Captain Dunbar's office was louder than usual. It seemed everyone was talking, that is everyone except Dunbar himself. He was sitting with his hands folded on the table watching his crew. Willa looked up mid-sentence and never finished that thought. "What's wrong, Cap?" she asked.

"Nothing." This seemed to be his standard answer to everything lately.

"Did you hear what we were saying? I think we are getting close to some answers. Also, I'd venture an educated guess that Luther probably saw something. And that something was what led to his death." Willa lowered her voice as she spoke.

Frank produced an enlarged copy of Luther's pictures from his phone. The outline of the small boat and the shadowy figures bent over it had new meaning now. However, the photos were unable to capture any registration number or name on the boat or any other identifying characteristics of the men or location.

The meeting lasted an hour but had put renewed vigor into this investigation. As everyone left the table, Captain motioned Willa to wait. She looked at him expectantly and sat back down. Russell glanced over his shoulder as Captain spoke to him, "Russell, shut the door."

Okay, he thought, maybe Willa was in trouble. Captain had been sitting at the head of the table, now he moved closer to her. Captain was a good man; he had worked here many years and had risen through the ranks. He believed in hard work and honesty and surrounded himself with people who shared his same values.

Lately, he had come under a lot of pressure, a lot of scrutiny and down-right harsh criticism of his leadership and his people. This wasn't the first time, but in the past, he had been able to satisfy the upper office, and prove his department was performing at a very acceptable rate. This wasn't the first murder and it wouldn't be the last. But, now he had two active cases and not a lot to show in the way of evidence.

Yesterday's meeting with his boss had taken a 180° turn. The mayor sat in as he had done before, but he had a lot to say this time. Most of it critical. His main focus had been with Willa. He never liked her and yesterday he issued an ultimatum. His argument was, she wasn't doing her job. Not only that, she was interviewing with a private investigation company looking for a change in location.

He did not say how he knew this, but he was well aware it was happening. This knocked Captain Dunbar for a loop. He thought Willa was the hardest working detective he had. He would have sworn she was satisfied here.

This was her home. She loved living and working here.

When Captain took the seat next to Willa, she knew something was up. He appeared haggard and he acted like his mind was going in a hundred different directions. This wouldn't be good. She was sure he didn't have the information she was grappling with...or did he? "Is there something you need to tell me?" he got right to the point.

Her mind couldn't accept how serious he seemed. "About what? I told you where we were, we are working as hard as possible. What do you mean?"

He turned to her and said, "Get out of here!"

She had never seen him so mad. At least not at her. He was her biggest fan. He had gone to bat for her many times. She tried to remember what that was like as she pushed back her chair. Quickly, she left the office. She didn't look up at anyone in the office as she made her way to the bathroom. She locked the door behind her, approached the sink and scanned her face in the mirror.

What she saw looking back surprised her. The face was red and blotchy, the eyes were damp, she was shaking. What was happening to her? Was she the same woman that walked into the office this morning with strong resolve? With a need to settle this case. The one which somehow was about her now. Had the captain been talking about her encounter with Paul Graves? How would he know?

She dried her eyes, shook her head and promised herself not to fall to pieces. She had work to do as long as she still had a job.

Barbara Marvin

Chapter 28

Jon's drive and composure surprised even him. Knowing Cole had spent a lot of time at Big Bart's, he decided to find out as much about that place as he could. And the owner. And frequent customers. He started with Big Bart himself, whose name was Barten Pressman. He had a license going back seven years. It had been transferred with the purchase of Tiger Bar, now known as Big Bart's. The broker had been J. Whitman.

At first glance everything seemed to be in order. Bart had acquired financing from a private lender and it was in order. No violations noted, no taxes unpaid, no other notations of any kind. Jon smirked to himself when he read that. A place like Big Bart's where fights broke out nightly, where strangers were given the option of being harassed or leaving, a place where very few were welcome, would have been high on the radar of law enforcement.

Barten Pressman's application showed his hometown as a small town he had never heard of. He quickly pulled it up on the map and was surprised it was so close. He would check it out as soon as he had time to make the trip.

* * * * *

Willa's eyes were straight ahead. Not looking at anyone in the office. Especially Russ, who was staring a hole through her. Carefully pulling out the murder book, she wanted to go over everything again. The office was quiet, until Kevin spoke up.

"I just talked to my Dad... I told him I would get back to him. Do we have anything new to release? Anything at all? You know how he is."

"Well," Willa looked up. The whole office was looking at her. "There doesn't seem to be any connection between the two cases, unless you draw a line in the water. Let's go over this again. Come on guys."

"Are you Okay?" Russ asked with definite concern in his voice.

"Yes, I'm fine. Thanks for asking."

Kevin didn't know whether to chime in or keep quiet, so for once he kept his mouth closed.

And then she laughed. They all laughed with her, but it wasn't over. Their worries were evident.

* * * * *

Jon and Earl needed to talk. To compare ideas and notes. If Jon were a betting man, he would bet the farm that the answers would involve Big Bart's. They met for lunch at the Marina. Neither one was hungry, but this was out of the way and they needed privacy. "We need to take a short trip," Jon stated as soon as the waitress left their table.

Earl looked out over the beautiful blue waters, rolling in in perfect rhythm. "Where to?" he said turning to face Jon. The look on Jon's face was determined, serious. More serious than Earl has seen in the past.

In his notebook, Jon had outlined a plan.

"Jon, you are doing a lot of work on this. You know this is what your Dad is paying me for." Earl informed him.

"Yes, I do, and I want to be aware of anything and everything you find. We can cover more ground together."

Earl nodded, he liked this guy. "I'm still trying to get some info from Big Bart's. Do you realize that place is creepy; I'm from Chicago so you don't hear me say that often. As soon as I opened the door, I thought I heard banjos playing."

Jon laughed. "Yeah, you probably did. I'm taking the rest of the day off; I thought we could take a ride."

"I'm game! Where to?" Earl replied.

*　*　*　*　*

Jon and Earl were taking a ride to a small town known as Duette. Using Earl's rental car seemed like a better idea than using Jon's red Lexus. There probably weren't many red Lexus Sports cars in Duette.

Neither of them knew what to expect. Jon had done some research online and wasn't surprised to find out Earl had, too. Coming from two different points, they both ended up thinking they needed to check out Duette. The surprise was learning two local Sarasota citizens were from there, one who was already on their radar. The next step would be to find a connection. Maybe between Sarasota and Duette; maybe between the two men who once lived in Duette. The ride took them north over the Manatee River. In their research, they had learned of the vineyards and winery. They also knew that Duette had an elementary school. The school was permanently closed and was now being considered as a historical site. It had been the last one-teacher elementary school in Florida. Jon and Earl had smiled. "That must have been something; can you imagine one teacher for 6 grades!" pondered Earl, remembering his own schooling.

The information obtained from Google had been limited, but they were determined to see where this would lead them. "I'm sure they knew each other. As kids. Growing up!" Jon stated as they cruised through one small town at a time.

"Yeah, it would be hard not to. They were close in age… Although, they seem to have different lives."

"Maybe one doesn't know the other lived here? What are the odds of that in such a small town?"

They were quiet for a time. Jon's mind was focused on the issues he had learned about Detective Dupree's encounters with the Chicago firm and the huge push to get her on board. He was a little surprised to learn she wasn't taking it personally. She was considering it a farce to get her out of the picture. "You seemed to have made a good impression on the investigators' office," Jon said to Earl, still frowning.

"Yes, but I'd like to be in on all the conversations."

"Well, keep working … maybe with what we learn today, you will have something to negotiate with."

Both were quiet. The GPS interrupted the moment with instructions to turn right on

State Road 62. "I think we are almost there," Earl interjected.

"Think again, it's still a ways to go," Jon responded. Turning east on 62 didn't bother Jon, but Earl seemed to look around, wondering where everyone went. The area was very rural. A lot of farms with not much of anything else. No wonder anyone with any ambition other than farming would leave the area. Jon was keeping up with the idle chatter just to see if Earl understood Florida. Coming from Chicago, often influenced your view of how the other half lives. And Florida seems to be different all around. Of course, the one-room schoolhouse was out there even for Florida. Speaking of schools, Jon could see the school in the distance.

"Slow down. I think this is it," Jon directed.

"There are cars parked in front," Earl replied, surprised.

"Pull in, let's see what's going on."

Earl turned slowly onto the gravel drive and parked next to a Ford truck.

"If the school is closed, I doubt they would still have records here, but it doesn't hurt to ask," Jon stated as he put on his press badge. Maybe he would get further with the questioning if it seemed like his interest was in the school and not the past attendees. The school door opened, and Jon and Earl got their first look at the friendly face of their new informant.

They had their story straight. Jon had his press badge on and Earl was carrying a Nikon camera. A must for a journalist looking to enhance his story. Before they exited the car, Jon had given Earl a quick lesson on how to use it. Earl was good with cameras. He had just never used one this expensive. If possible, they would be taking home information that could be useful to this case.

Jon's heart still ached thinking of his friend, Cole. Thinking he was getting closer to answers helped him. "Hello," Jon said holding out his hand. "My name is Jon Albee from the Sentinel Press.

"Hi, I'm Zack. Looks like you guys are here to learn a few things about our local project."

"This is Earl – my partner. We are here to learn all we can."

"Good, come on in. I'll let you talk to Martha, she's in charge."

Earl was busy taking pictures and quite surprised by the friendly atmosphere.

Barbara Marvin

Chapter 29

This would be a very long day. He couldn't turn the news off. It was like he was tied to the television. The newspapers had carried the story on the front page, complete with photos and biographical information about Cole. This was totally out of hand. As on edge as he was, he was more affected by what he anticipated was on the horizon for him.

His phone had not vibrated with the expected call. His doorbell had not chimed. His cousin had been quiet. However, he knew the fallout was on its way. This time he would be better prepared. Sometimes things made a big splash – why use that word now, he thought? He could wait it out. It was big and loud, but nothing to connect him and his cousin to anything going on.

His third cup of coffee was almost too much. He thought back to when this all began. To his need to purchase the property. It seemed like a good thing at the time; an easy transaction with a little help from his cousin. How it all started to go south after the bank loan, which was the first thing with strings attached. Then he needed a license. He should have known Jeff Whitman wasn't doing this for nothing. Then, Jeff put his future on the line by threatening the Mayor. If he thought the Mayor would just pay up, he had another thought coming.

Funny how nothing is ever easy.

His cousin had more to lose than he did; that's why he had recorded their last meeting. He wasn't as dumb as Sid had assumed. His cousin had thought he had the upper hand. Let's see how he gets out of this? Tonight would be crucial.

* * * * *

Willa was the first one in the office. Today she had a lot on her plate; she needed to get started before anyone interrupted her. She had become a law enforcement officer for a reason. That reason was more evident than ever now. One thing she learned early in life was that everyone wasn't always who they seemed. Her dad was the most obvious case. He had portrayed himself, to everyone but her mother and herself, as a good guy. Law abiding, good provider, an upstanding sort. That wasn't who he was at all. Her home life had been filled with abuse on all levels. Her mother was a victim. Even when an abuser dies the weight of having endured it never really leaves, thought Willa. It only buries itself deeper, allowing victims to delude themselves into thinking that all is well now. Recovery takes a long time. She was still working on it.

Her eyes focused on her computer. The picture she was looking at was looking back at her. It could have been her father. Not the physical image, she saw through that. No, it was far more volatile than that. She read on, sometimes escaping, moving to a new town meant a chance to start over. For some people it gave them opportunities to hide the evil person that would eventually raise its ugly head again. Now she knew why she was in the crosshairs. She prepared her evidence, and when Captain Dunbar walked in she would grab him. The sooner he knew the truth, the sooner she would be safe.

It was now obvious to Willa that Luther had been in the wrong place at the wrong time. Life isn't fair; all he wanted to do was catch a few fish. Instead, he witnessed something so outrageous it got him killed. Reading Cole's novel last night kept her mesmerized. All she had to do was fill in the names, the actual names, like names of the current citizens and she had the answers. When it hit her at last, it seemed so easy.

Poor Cole, if he had written things a little differently, he would probably still be alive. If he had elected to be creative and add, his own version of the events, the outcome would be different.

Captain Dunbar walked right past her desk; he didn't even look at her or say hello. As he unlocked his office, his shoulders slumped. He looked awful even though he had no idea what this day had in store for him; or did he? Russell, Kevin, and Frank walked into the office at the same time, loud and revved.

"Willa," Russel called out, smiling, "you are early – what's new?"

"A lot," she answered, looking at him. Her smile was a little forced. However, anytime she could, she smiled at him; it made her day. "I think Captain Dunbar is ready for us," she added, pointing to his office.

The door to Captain's office was open. Willa tapped on it as she entered, followed by Russell, Frank, and Kevin. Kevin gently shut the door behind him, as everyone took their seats. Today, the atmosphere at the table had changed. Usually everyone was speaking at once and Captain had to take control. The look on his face today had everyone quiet.

"Today isn't like any other day; today you will see some very big changes in our department," Captain spoke slowly, measuring each word.

"Captain" Willa stated.

"Willa, please be quiet."

"Captain, I have something we all need to hear," she blurted out.

"Not now!" If looks could kill, she would be a goner. So, she just sat there to wait it out. Wondering what was eating Dunbar.

"As your Captain, it is my responsibility to evaluate the job you are doing, the effort you are exerting. The results you are getting. Not all crimes can be solved," he paused, looking around the table. First at Kevin, then Frank and Russell. Lastly at Willa. The room was quiet; this sounded like the start of a very bad motivational meeting; only that wasn't Captain's style.

"I've been informed that … changes are about to occur," again, he paused. "Some of us will no longer be working here."

Everyone started at once. "What do you mean?" Russell was the loudest. "Which ones?" said Kevin. Frank and Willa's comments were drowned out.

When Willa finally came to her senses, she decided she could not be quiet. "Captain, before you go any further, could I say a few words?" she asked, pulling a file from beneath the stack of papers in front of her.

"Okay but make it short. I have somewhere to be," he answered.

She began to pass out sheets of paper to everyone. Certain lines were highlighted. "Look at this," she started.

"Wait a minute," Captain interrupted staring at the sheets she had given out. "This is a cold case. We have no time for this."

"Yes, we do. Please, bear with me." As they read the first page, Willa explained, "What you are reading is from our very own reports. A lot of it wasn't released to the public."

Captain interrupts, "Where are you going with this?"

"I have something that might be the answer to this cold case and the current case we are struggling with."

"This had better be good," Captain stated.

Willa called attention to the handout. She had underlined certain lines and places on a number of pages. Her second handout wasn't from their files, but pages from Cole's book, *The Murder Book*. "If you will notice, the names have been changed, but only the names. Cole was actually rewriting this case. At least it seems that way. He had no access to our files and we did not release all the details he has here."

Everyone now had the copies side by side. Captain had calmed down a little, but not much. Willa was focused on what she had discovered, not what was driving the Captain.

All at once she stopped. It dawned on her what Captain Dunbar had said, some of us will no longer be here! What did that mean? Was it her? Who else had come under scrutiny, lately? "Captain," she said, "I'm sorry I got carried away. I ..." she sat down and put her hands on the sides of her face. The look on Captain's face told her something was happening, and it had nothing to do with this case or the cold case.

Chapter 30

Jon and Earl remained at Duette for the better part of the afternoon. Everyone was helpful and eager to offer their own personalized version of local history. The school was opened in 1930 and known as a strawberry school, due to its April to December school year; that meant school was closed during the strawberry harvest. During its early years, students were also allowed to miss school in order to work at harvest time for other crops. We were informed that after many meetings, the school would become a museum. Their tour inside done, Jon and Earl felt they had been given firsthand knowledge of what it must have been like growing up here.

They learned that this was Manatee County and that's where the school records were. An older woman looking as if lost in nostalgia entered the room. "Excuse me, my name is Jon Albee. I'm a journalist with the Sarasota Sentential," Jon smiled and held out his hand. She quickly grasped it with both of hers.

"Hi, Jon. I'm Greta Long. I was a teacher here fifteen years ago. How do you like the place," she smiled, and Jon could see she was very proud of what was going on. "I haven't taught here for years; and I wanted to be here, this was something so special. They let me sit here and answer questions," she laughed. "I taught Zack there, so he has to be respectful."

Jon's eyes turned toward the tall man in a blue workman's uniform. Zack smiled. "Can I ask you a few questions, Ms. Long," Jon inquired. There was nowhere to sit, so he continued to stand. It didn't bother him, he had done interviews this way many times.

"Ms. Long, do you remember a man named Sidney Sullivan?"

"Oh, yes, but I have to remind you, he was in elementary school when I taught him. I am so glad he matured, went on to high school and college. I understand he is doing a great job in your town as a mayor."

Jon smiled, "Yes, he seems to be. Tell me a little about him, if you don't mind." Jon was trying to be as focused on her as he could be; his mind was in high gear, hoping he had hit the mother lode of information.

"Well, you know his dad was a sharecropper, and not the best around. Sidney worked on the farm, even when he was in elementary school," she paused. "Maybe that's why he went on to college, to get away from this life."

"Did he have other abilities in school?"

"Oh, yes, my goodness. He and his cousin – let me see, I can't remember his name."

"Could it be Bart?" Jon guessed.

"Yes, you are right! I don't know whatever happened to him. He was a, how can I say this nicely? He was a juvenile delinquent, always in trouble, always creating a disturbance in class."

Jon was feeling quite proud of the fact that interviewing Ms. Long was easy; she was in a nostalgic mood. Maybe it was the location, maybe the fact that she was just the talkative mood. Either way, as soon as they could fact check them, he was sure he had the start of a very interesting story.

* * * * *

No one said a word. Captain Dunbar pushed back his chair and stood up. It was as if the chair and the table were on fire. His face was flushed, his eyes focused on the wall in front of him. After a brief moment, he cleared his throat.

"I want you, all of you here, to be the first to know. At the end of this week, I will be leaving; retiring. I will be moving out of town. It has been a pleasure ..."

"Captain, what are you saying," Russell interrupted him. "You are leaving your job? Who's taking your place? Why? What's going on? Are you ill? Are you ... what, just like that – leaving?"

Willa found it hard to comprehend what came out of Cap's mouth. "Captain, this is sudden. What brought it on? Could you tell us that?" she finally blurted out.

"It's personal. I know you all will continue to do a great job, and whoever is tapped to replace me, will inherit a great group of officers," he continued to speak. Willa couldn't believe it. It all sounded rehearsed, like he had spent a lot of time planning what to say. And maybe, what not to say.

After another ten minutes, Captain's oratory seemed to fade as he looked around the table. He closed his mouth and started to leave the room.

"Wait," Willa quickly commanded. "Don't go. We are not through here!"

He stopped, looked at her, and replied, "I'm through."

"No, that's not true. I have something to present to all of you." She held up one of the sheets of paper she had been passing out before she was so heartrendingly interrupted. Now it was her turn. Regardless of what Captain Dunbar had just said, she wasn't buying it. And after her presentation, maybe he wouldn't either.

"Last night it all connected!" she picked up where she left off. "If you look at the first and third sheets, side-by-side, you will see that Cole's book parallels exactly, the incident and evidence in the cold case of Jefferson Whitman, even facts not disclosed to the public."

Willa went on to lay out each and every item that was a part of Cole's book. The excitement around the table was noticeable, except for Captain. He just sat there as if in a trance. "Willa, do you know what you are saying?" asked Russell.

"Yes, I do. Do you know what this means?" she replied.

"We have our work cut out for us," Kevin piped up.

Frank was busy making notes for himself. This changed everything, as far as the detectives were concerned. Frank looked up, "This is the motive. Cole was killed because he knew too much. He wanted a best seller, so he wrote something that he would have been safer keeping quiet about."

"I bet Luther saw something involving Cole's encounter with his end," Kevin added.

Captain's demeanor had changed. He was looking at each of his detectives. A smile was forming on his face. "You all are so smart. I think you have the answers to a lot of questions on my mind," he said.

Suddenly, the atmosphere had changed. Things might be closer to home than any of them could imagine.

Barbara Marvin

Chapter 31

It was early when Earl and Jon converged on the sheriff's office. "Good morning, June," Jon said. "We called Lisa, she is expecting us." Lisa rose from her desk and met both men. After Jon thanked her for allowing them to come in so early, she ushered them into a conference room.

"As I mentioned, the detectives are still in their meeting. It should be breaking up soon," Lisa informed them.

"We'll wait," Jon and Earl said in unison.

"If you need me, I'll be right outside," she said. She closed the door behind her allowing Jon and Earl a little privacy.

The men had been up most of the night. They had done a good job of linking the info they had, concerning the book and the cold case. Of course, they didn't have information that wasn't released to the public, but it seems the book included that information. They had a lot of notes to compare with the detectives. They had gotten info from Delaware about the LLC on the Siesta Key property, after learning Sid Sullivan was the president.

Late yesterday Earl had ventured onto the property to check it out. He pretended to be interested in buying it. No one was there, so he was able to park in the drive some distance from the house. The drive had an ornate gate with a large padlock restricting cars from entering.

As was common with many homes in the area, the gate did not prohibit foot traffic from entering the property. So, Earl had parked in the drive and walked about 20 feet to go around the gate, towards the home. The home was more like a mansion than a house. It was a two-story red structure with a portico in front and a veranda in the back. Earl did not think the home was being used, but it was in pristine shape. He wondered what it would bring on the open market. There was no doubt it was way beyond his means, and he was pretty well off. However, he wasn't focusing on the value, he was searching for evidence that a crime may have been committed here.

If this was where Cole had been brought, before or after his death, the only way out of the place without being seen would be on the water. Searching the ground in front of the garage, he was encouraged to see footprints and scuff marks that looked fresh. They would all disappear if the forecasted rain occurred. Earl pulled out his phone and took pictures.

He walked towards the dock. The cobbled-stone path held no evidence; but it led to the boat launch beside the dock. That was a different story. He took more pictures. As he stepped on the dock, he heard a shout.

"Hey," loud and clear. He ignored it and pretended to be looking up and down the bay. Actually, he saw something dark on the dock itself. Quickly, he took a picture and slipped his phone in his front pocket.

"Hey, you. Did you know you are trespassing?" the voice was right on him now.

Earl turned and was looking at a man in his forties with dark brown hair, about six feet tall, maybe two hundred fifty pounds. Not some one you wanted to argue with; someone trying to look friendly, but unable to camouflage his aggression.

"Oh, hi, I'm Earl, just looking at this place. I'm thinking about moving here and I am out this morning looking at properties that I might want to put an offer on. This place sounded perfect, but the actual property is a little off from the listing. I guess that isn't unusual for real estate listings," Earl babbled on trying to distract the man and setting up the background so his excuse of being at the wrong address would seem credible.

"This place isn't for sale," the man said smiling.

"This is 7761 Midnight Pass Road, right?" Earl questioned.

"No, it isn't. I'm the grounds keeper and you shouldn't be here."

"Sorry, my mistake. I apologize. I must have the wrong address. Guess that explains the listing being different."

"You are definitely at the wrong address!"

"I love this place. I was just thinking I probably couldn't afford it, but, boy would I love to live here. Do you live here?"

"No, I'm the grounds keeper, I told you. You need to leave, now."

"Okay, honest mistake. I meant no harm; have a good day," Earl said walking quickly towards his car.

He could see this grounds keeper was carrying a concealed weapon. Earl turned and waved as he got in his car. He took a picture of the truck parked next to his car as he backed out and another of the license plate. He hoped this would be enough to identify the man.

He pulled out and headed north. The smile he had plastered on his face was gone. He was meeting Jon at Marina Bar and made the trek in record time. He backed into a parking space and waited for the grounds keeper to pass. Within a few minutes he saw him speed by. He and Jon had a lot to discuss.

Chapter 32

His phone buzzed. The phone. Oh no! Here it comes. "Yes," he answered rather quietly, even though no one was around.

"Tonight, same place."

Before he could agree, the phone went dead. The caller had already hung up. Tonight would be the fix. They needed a plan. It seemed as if the previous plan had not worked; so, something more permanent had to occur. He turned off the television and threw the newspaper in the trash. He couldn't focus on a solution with all that noise going on.

* * * * *

Lisa immediately started talking as the detectives left Captain Dunbar's office. "I have two visitors in conference room number two," she said.

"Who are they?" Russell asked.

"Journalist Jon and his PI Earl!" she replied.

"No, no time for them now," Russell added, looking at Willa.

"I think you all need to hear them out. You can always walk out, come on Russell. I told them they could see you," Lisa pleaded.

"Okay, this had better be good," Russell said nodding to Kevin, Willa, and Frank.

"When did they get here?" Willa asked.

"About twenty minutes ago. They have been waiting for your meeting to end."

"Thanks, Lisa," Willa added trying to keep the sarcasm out of her voice as they headed to the conference room thinking maybe this would be a good thing. Maybe Jon and Earl might have answers to some of the questions foremost in her mind.

An hour later as Willa and the guys put all the information from Earl and Jon together, the detectives walked out of the room. She was amazed at what was obvious. Everything was falling into place. Now she knew who and why someone was pursuing her and why Captain was being replaced. All that was about to change.

This would be a very sensitive situation. They prepared the necessary probable cause items for the court. It was easy once they had the background data laid out. As soon as the judge was available, the day would move fast. They set up their schedule; everything must happen at the same time. They would search the mayor's home and the home of his cousin, Big Bart, at the same time.

They debated whether to do a late-night raid or wait till early morning. They decided they couldn't wait until tomorrow. Paul Graves, the man trying to recruit her would be at Lonnie's tonight and when she didn't show, his first response would be to his employer. Thereby alerting him that things were happening.

As things stood now, they would arrest him first to keep him from alerting anyone as they carried out their search warrants and arrests warrants.

Chapter 33

Big Bart's trip to Duette seemed to take forever. His mind was trying to grasp where they had gone wrong. How they had become targets of law enforcements. Even though Cole had used everything he heard about the original crime, his book was fiction. No names were the same. How anyone could tie what he wrote to an unsolved murder years ago was hard for him to believe. After all, if law enforcement had not been able to figure it out then, how had the book given them information they needed. They had been so careful. They hired only out of town help for the dirty work.

Lars, for example. He came in, tended bar for a couple nights, did his job, and left. It was obvious he was not a local, so it was not a big stretch to say this was not what he was looking for. It was the perfect cover for him. Even when they had to remove Jefferson Whitman. The men they brought in assumed the role of interested investors looking for property. There were dozens of men and women coming to this city to buy property. They didn't stand out. Things had been good for so long. What could they do now?

He was almost to the turn-off at State Road 62, a smile temporarily grazed his face. It used to be when he reached this point, he was almost home and the feeling overwhelmed him. He was capable of making it anywhere, without looking back. And he was afraid he wouldn't be coming back, ever. He wasn't filled with nostalgia only anger and angst. As usual, the traffic was almost non-existent at this point.

A few more miles on a lonesome stretch of road and he would be home. He had made up his mind, he would just disappear. He would leave from here. Never look back. He had nothing to hold him. His clothes were all packed and his car was gassed up. He had withdrawn his money from the local bank and his other accounts were in several other cities under other names. It wouldn't be that hard.

He was going to miss Sarasota, and of course, his bar. But all good things must come to an end. He wasn't sure if he would miss his cousin or not. Sid had used his position in government to line his pockets pretty darn good. While his cousin did help him from time to time, it seemed like Sydney benefited from their relationship way more than he did. As he neared the old school house, he could see a car parked in the lot. His cousin was early; that was a very bad sign.

Barbara Marvin

Chapter 34

Jon and Earl seemed to work together quite well. However, tonight Jon was operating as the journalist and Earl as a PI. Jon expected to get a good story out of this and most importantly, find justice for his friend Cole. The very thought that Cole was gone, no more fishing trips, no more comparing notes about that last girlfriend, no more nights at Big Bart's together. And after this, maybe, no more Big Bart's. It hurt to his very soul. It had left an impact on him and he was intent on seeing that some good come out of this situation.

They headed out to Lonnie's, to see the beginning of the end. Pulling into the parking lot, Earl pointed to Paul's car. A lot with this much light was a bonus tonight. Jon took a picture of the car, including the license plate and Earl phoned the number in to his sources. They needed to know who Graves was, who he was working for.

Jon and Earl would take on the role as regulars at the bar. It worked for them.

As they entered, they noisily greeted Lonnie, and took a seat at a table near the door. They would be able to prevent Graves from leaving, if it became necessary. Looking around they saw him sitting alone. He had arrived early and sat with his back to the wall, facing the front door. Jon wondered if he had done this to prevent Willa from facing the door as she always did.

"Thanks, Lonnie," Earl said as she placed their drinks on the table. She was also carrying out her part. Everyone was aware something was up. Everyone except Graves. He continued to nurse his drink and sit with a satisfied smirk on his face. Tonight would be his last night in town. As soon as Willa agreed to take the Chicago job, he would be on the next plane to O'Hare.

This job paid very well, and he was satisfied he had done a good job. Leaving here he would drive to Tampa for his flight. Sarasota had limited flights and there were no nonstops to his destination tonight, so that airport was out.

Since his boss was paying, he was going first class. Expecting to be in the Windy City by midnight, he would have a few days before his next job, in Boston. Oh well, he didn't mind the cold weather. The next job involved a Boston business man. He wondered what name he should use there.

Willa pushed open the door and slowly glanced around the room, pretending to look for Paul. She had already been informed exactly where he was sitting by a call from Lonnie. After noticing Jon and Earl, her eyes settled on Paul Graves and she displayed a large smile. She waved and headed towards him.

She made no comment about his seat and greeted him warmly, as he rose and offered his hand. Lonnie brought Willa a drink and Paul another. "Thanks," Willa said to Lonnie. Waiting until Lonnie was out of ear range, she leaned in to Paul and said, "How are you tonight?"

"Fine, now that you are here," he replied, unable to keep his voice serious.

"That's good," she paused. "Because you are under arrest for aiding and abetting a felony, solicitation of a law enforcement officer, and there are probably a few more charges that will be added as the night progresses. Please stand up."

"What, what the hell is going on?"

Before he could push back from the table to stand, Russell was at his side.

"Make this easy or make it hard. Your choice." Willa informed him.

His face, no longer wearing that smug smile, looked a little haggard.

Chapter 35

The officers assigned to watch the mayor and the bar owner both reported in about the same time. Both suspects had left, Big Bart left the bar and Sid Sullivan left his home around the same time. Using unmarked cars to follow them had been easy.

Neither man seemed aware they were under scrutiny. But they stayed within the speed limit as they headed to 301, just a couple of miles apart. Traffic was not heavy, but was steady, helping the unmarked cars to blend in with traffic. As the officers checked in with each other they both came to the realization that soon it wouldn't be possible to remain unseen. They had an idea where this was heading.

The first car decided to pull ahead and pass Bart's truck. Picking up speed, he continued on until Highway 62 was in sight. Making a right turn he increased his speed to put more space between himself and the bar owner to avoid being noticed. It was important not to be seen. Two other cars on this lonely stretch of road would arouse suspicion.

On 62 there weren't many places to pull off and wait. Both sides of the highway were plowed fields that would soon be strawberries, tomatoes and other local crops. He passed Duette School; had the spot light not been shining on the flag blowing in the breeze he would have missed it. A short distance later he pulled off the road at a very small convenience store that was closed. Watching the road, the only traffic was the other officer which pulled in beside him and got out.

"Where are they?" the first officer asked.

"They both pulled in at the school house."

"Okay, I'll call it in" the first officer responded.

Chapter 36

The detectives had been informed that their two men of interest had both left the city and were being followed by assisting agents. Maybe this is better. They had notified the nearby county of their impending action and the local law enforcement had offered any help they might need.

Bart was now sitting in Sid's car, both men were uneasy. Sid was angry, and Bart was trying to calm him down. "They have nothing on us," Bart informed his cousin.

"Then why do I think this is getting so close?"

"You're paranoid! Calm down, let's think this through."

Sid, who was known for his direct approach and his superior manner wasn't living up to his reputation. Tonight he was sweating and looking for answers. "You said you were getting rid of that female detective and the Captain. That was a start. That will slow down the process of the open cases a lot. Maybe even cause them to go cold... like the Whitman thing." Bart explained.

Sid just put his head in his hands and groaned.

"I should never have trusted you to do what I told you to. You were never good at following directions." Sid said.

"Come on Sid. I did everything by the book, everything you told me to. The Whitman thing is old. I don't think they can connect the two."

"You better hope they can't."

Bart looked up just as a local patrol car pulled in to the school drive.

"Oh my God, what's this?" Sid gasped.

"Calm down, I'll handle it," Bart interjected.

"No, leave it to me," Sid insisted.

The patrolman got out of his car, very impassive, but very composed. He didn't look like a threat at all.

"Good evening officer," Sid said as the officer bent down and looked in the car.

"Could I see your driver's license, please."

"Sure, what's the trouble?"

Sid removed his license from his wallet and handed it to the officer along with his business card.

"Mr. Sullivan, I'm sorry to bother you. I thought you all were a couple of kids out here, up to no good. Here, take your license," he paused and then added, "Why are you out here anyway?"

"Just reminiscing. My cousin and I went to this school, years ago. Heard it had closed. Hope they don't tear it down."

"No need to worry about that. It will soon be a museum," replied the officer. "I suggest you come back during the daytime. The museum isn't open yet, but you could still look around. It is open during the day while people are here getting it ready. Have a good evening."

The officer returned to his car. He called on a private line, in case the men in the car had police scanners. He told the officer who was waiting down the road at the convenience store that the men in the car were the ones they were looking for.

Before Bart could think of what he could say to calm Sid down, four unmarked squad cars converged on the drive, surrounding the mayor and his cousin, blocking their exit.

The detectives jumped from their car with guns drawn.

"Out of the car! Out of the car! Now!"

Sid and Bart got out of the car with hands raised. "What's the problem, officer? We were just leaving. Ask the patrolman," said Bart.

Pulling out handcuffs, the closest officer said, "Hands behind your back! Now! You have the right to remain silent ..."

Chapter 37

It had been an extremely long night. Of course, the mayor and his cousin lawyered up right away. But the evidence found at their homes was very incriminating.

They found proof of ownership for the three houses on Siesta Key belonging to Sid. They even found a connection to Jefferson Whitman; his pistol was in Sid's collection. It was considered an antique and Sid couldn't pass it up. It rounded out his Civil War era collection. It was a Smith & Wesson Russian Revolver made in the early 1870's, with a nickel finish and ivory grips. After Whitman's death it was listed as stolen. There were other indications that Sid was involved in his death.

With Sid and Bart in jail, the work of the department was cut out for them. Paul Graves had admitted he had been hired by Sid to entice Willa to Chicago. That wasn't a crime. But they needed him to testify at a later date. He readily agreed. While he knew everything was not on the up and up, he insisted that he would not have become involved in something that was definitely illegal. Especially something that was to coverup a murder.

Jon interviewed Paul as soon as he was released. Willa agreed to give Jon a story after things died down. He was elated. Willa had never shared anything with him, everything he needed went through Lisa. Maybe, he dreamed, this would be the beginning of more open sharing with the police department. That would go a long way to helping him in his career.

Lisa was busy adding new photos and stories to the bulletin board. As always, she wanted to share with the public the positive things and successes that were happening at the department. As long as she was around, no one would ever be able to say they were unaware of the good things happening within the department. She was working very hard with Jon on another subject. Educating the public about the need for a cold case department. This would be a win for both the department and the newspaper – fostering Jon's hope for open sharing.

Captain Dunbar's job was no longer in jeopardy, thanks to all the work that had been accomplished. He was now able to feel pride in his department and the people who worked in that department, knowing they were as good as he gave them credit for being.

Earl insisted Willa have dinner with him before he departed, she agreed and was actually looking forward to it. Who knows, maybe she didn't need to leave Florida to find someone she could enjoy spending time with. Earl hoped it could be the start of something big, some reason to return to the Sunshine State in the near future.

Jon planned to accompany Earl to Chicago, just to see his father and say "thanks". It was the least he could do.

Everyone expected Cole's Murder Book to reach the best seller list. They wouldn't be wrong.

Barbara Marvin

Made in the USA
Coppell, TX
17 April 2020